MISADVENTURE

STORIES

A
STRANGE
OBJECT
Austin, Texas

Misadventure

Nicholas Grider

The stories in this collection have appeared in slightly different form in the following journals:

"Millions of Americans Are Strange" in *Guernica*, "Disappearing Act" in *Bare Fiction*, "Formers (An Index)" in *Caketrain*, "Misadventure" in *Conjunctions*, "Liars" in *Milk*, "Nightfall" in *Hobart*, and "This Is Not a Romance" in the *Blue Lake Review*.

Published by
A Strange Object
astrangeobject.com

ISBN 978-0-9892759-3-4

Cover design by Rodrigo Corral Design / Rachel Adam
Book design by Amber Morena

FOR JEANNE MARIE GRIDER

CONTENTS

There are more people who wish to be loved than there are who are willing to love.

—NICOLAS CHAMFORT

MILLIONS OF AMERICANS
ARE STRANGE

Millions of Americans do strange or extreme things without quite being able to articulate why. Gary can't quite
articulate why he does a lot of things. When George ties
Gary to the chair, he promises Gary he won't get bored.
On the phone, George reassures his former lover Allen
that their breakup had nothing to do with Allen never
wanting to go anywhere or do anything. Allen is an ago-
raphobic. Agoraphobia is a condition that can be debilitat-
ing and affects millions of Americans. Sometimes people
from all walks of life can be afraid that if they go out into
the throng they might somehow vanish. Millions of Americans disappear every year and are never found and after

long periods are presumed dead. Hannah has a suitcase with some clothes and documents and her passport in it under her bed but always decides to wait. Hannah always waits to disappear because she wants to take care of Hank. Hank is a functional alcoholic. Millions of Americans die each year from complications from alcoholism. Derek is an alcoholic whose favorite cover song is Jeff Buckley's cover of Leonard Cohen's "Hallelujah," and when he gets drunk, he sometimes asks Kelly to tie him to a kitchen chair and break his throne and cut his hair. Ramon and Walter are stiff from being tied to chairs for so long. When you are tied to a chair, your arms can be tied in front of you, down at your sides, or behind the chair back, which is the most uncomfortable for the person being tied, but is the most common technique because it is the most difficult to escape from. Frank is a heating and cooling sales rep with an unknowing wife and daughter. Frank pays John to meet him at a hotel when Frank is in town so John can tie him up and leave him alone like that for eight to ten hours. Frank knows John from bumping into him a few times at sales strategies seminars and then talking a little bit over drinks. John lives with his boyfriend, Frederick. Frederick is strikingly handsome. Men who are strikingly handsome have been found to be more financially successful at work than plain or ugly men. Harold is a plain man who invests a lot of money in clothing, including tailored suits, shirts, ties, pocket squares, tie bars, and cuff links, as well as shoes and socks. After a period during which formal business wear was on the wane, millions of Americans are returning to suits and ties in an effort to look more polished and confident. James makes an effort to look polished and confident, though he isn't very successful at it. James lives alone. Millions of Americans live alone. Sometimes this is by choice, and sometimes it is because a loved one has died or children have moved out, for example. Sandra lives just with her cats, Whiskers and Riley. Both of her children moved out when they went to college out of state, but Jane leaves their bedrooms as they were when Ella and Ava left because she knows in the current economic climate they may have to return. In the current economic climate, millions of Americans are without jobs. Lisa doesn't have a job. Lisa went to school for marketing but lost her job when the corporation told its workers it had to make cuts because of the current economic climate. Millions of Americans are suffering due to the current economic climate. Sometimes persons without jobs receive unemployment insurance while they look for new jobs. Jason receives unemployment insurance because he was laid off when the plant closed. Jason lives with his wife, Carol, and his son, Jack. Jack is three years old. Millions of Americans are three years old. Three-year-olds are still too socially and mentally underdeveloped to be capable of making moral judgments. When you make a moral judgment, you have to decide not just what's best for you but what's right and wrong for you and the people around you, either people you know or strangers or both. Millions of Americans are strangers. Lily and Uta are strangers to each other even though they live in the same apartment complex. Uta plays bass in a punk-funk band called the Watchtower. *The Watch-*

tower is a tract delivered door to door by Jehovah's Witnesses. Jehovah's Witnesses believe that millions now living will never die. Millions of Americans die every year. Ellen dies of heart failure. Ellen's cousin Kenneth almost dies of lymphoma. Lymphoma is a form of cancer that affects the lymph nodes. Lymph nodes are parts of the human body that help the body ward off infection. Because Olivia's tonsils become infected so frequently, she decides to have them surgically removed. Millions of Americans have surgery each year. Richard has surgery to repair his left inguinal hernia that occurred after he tried to lift a divan so he could drag it to the dumpster. Millions of Americans use dumpsters as convenient means of trash disposal. Victor mixes his shredded bank statements with old pasta sauce and puts all of it in the dumpster. Shredding documents is a means of protecting against identity theft. Millions of Americans' identities are stolen every year. Kevin's identity was stolen, and it is taking him almost two years to recover money lost from all the fraudulent uses of his debit card. Millions of Americans now use debit cards instead of checks as a means of making payments. Each year, Drake pays Alan and his team $750 to kidnap him, drive him to a remote motel room, take away his phone and wallet and clothing, and leave him stranded there, bound, gagged, blindfolded, and naked. Millions of Americans are kidnapped every year. Millions of Americans are naked. Millions of Americans get tied to chairs at some point in their lives. Doug gets duct-taped to an office chair as a frat house prank. Millions of Americans are members of college fraternities. Hector wants to pledge to become a brother at a fraternity at his university but decides it isn't worth the hassle or harassment. Millions of Americans get harassed each year. Harassed people like Sandra often have to change their plans. Sandra sits on her bed very still and decides she's not going to buy the rifle after all. When Allen fires his rifle skyward at the shopping mall, it ruins many people's plans. Millions of Americans try their hardest to plan for the future, but things fall apart. Millions of Americans fall apart each year. Millions of Americans can't quite explain how they feel or why and don't know what to do about it. Millions of Americans try to connect the dots but can't. Millions of Americans have stopped trying. Millions of Americans don't give a shit. Millions of Americans cry quietly in the kitchen. Millions of Americans are still waiting. Millions of Americans just want to know what it feels like. Millions of Americans spend money on goods and services they keep secret. Millions of Americans keep secrets. Millions of Americans want clear instructions. Millions of Americans are afraid things are just going to go on like this forever. Millions of Americans are afraid. Millions of Americans want to say yes. Millions of Americans say yes. Millions of Americans wander out into the dark to stare at the night sky and wonder why. Millions of Americans will never know why what happens happens. Millions of Americans feel completely anonymous. Millions of Americans get so far away from themselves they can't find their way back. Millions of Americans hyperventilate in parked cars on sunny days. Millions of Americans just want an answer. Millions of Americans can't wait anymore. Millions of Americans tilt their heads back and close their eyes and scream. Millions of Americans don't even have a reason. Millions of Americans do.

SECTION ONE

DISAPPEARING ACT

This is everything I know and most of what I suspect.

The campaign that led John to meet Aidan was the Erickson one, the new one, the print campaign that was just a field of navy blue with the white text in Garamond—"We do the worrying(,) so you don't have to"—accompanied by the company logo in the lower right. Not hard copy to edit, except for the fact that Creative wanted a comma after "worrying" where there shouldn't be one, and after emails were exchanged John had gone downstairs to talk to Creative personally, and that's how he met Aidan.

The comma was eventually removed from the final ad, which didn't run until after John disappeared.

John and Aidan worked at Los Angeles-based advertising agency Gordon/Whackey. Gordon and Whackey were the names of the two company founders, Daniel Gordon (always around micromanaging operations) and Elizabeth Whackey (who was the one who had the deep pockets, did the business lunches, the figurehead, etc., etc.).

There was an instant connection between John and Aidan, people said. People stopped short of calling it love at first sight.

John was short and wiry with dark, closely cropped hair, and he was always dressed more formally and stylishly than was called for by his position at the agency, e.g., he wore ties, though usually tastefully patterned ties with tastefully patterned shirts in novel fabrics. With jeans and sneakers. Nothing that broke the lax Angeleno work code or looked too out of place.

His clothing looked expensive for a man with his kind of job and salary.

Not much is known about John's private life or history outside of Gordon/Whackey.

Stewart, for his part, was never a person to share much information about anything. Things close to his vest in school, always. We were friends but never close friends, and I'm not sure what our friendship meant.

Daniel Gordon was said to once have said about John, not in his presence, that he looked as if he belonged in Creative.

John was an editor and Aidan was newest on the team in Creative, and the company was large enough for things to be impersonal. Though there was a NYC Gordon/Whackey branch office, most of the operations happened at the Los Angeles HQ. While the atmosphere was friendly, the place was expansive enough for people to walk by each other and smile and nod but not necessarily know each other's names.

John's disappearance was preceded by some erratic behavior, but it took nearly a week of unexplained absence before HR tried contacting him without success.

I'm not quite sure John ever really existed.

There was much discussion at the start of things whether it should be Gordon Whackey or Gordon/Whackey because of potential confusion over whether it was one name or two, and Whackey Gordon was out because of the pronunciation of Whackey, a name of Cornish derivation, and they had eventually settled on the pragmatic slash mark.

John's erratic behavior included talking to himself and writing his own ad copy and substituting it for what Creative did. He also had several verbal confrontations with Aidan over work issues the week of his disappearance.

John had worked as a copyeditor at Gordon/Whackey for three years before the unnecessary comma skirmish, coming over from Paulson in downtown LA to Gordon/Whackey in Glendale. John told Stewart (which I guess means they knew each other) the reasons for the move were the pay increase, the promotion in title, and the better commute because, after graduating from UCLA, he had moved to Eagle Rock and could just drive down Colorado to Brand and turn north instead of taking San Fernando into downtown with everyone else.

John was most struck, he said, by Aidan's green eyes. Not hazel, but a deep, saturated green.

Conjecture: Stewart actually doesn't know what color Aidan's eyes are or what John thought of them.

Common conjecture: John and Aidan's intense relationship, the hushed nature of it, and the evident deterioration of it had something to do with John's disappearance.

According to rumors at work, John disappeared not just from his job but entirely. Stewart told me he thought he saw police detectives talking first to the heads (i.e., Gordon, Whackey, John's supervisor, and HR) and then to Aidan in the glass-walled conference room.

Stewart wouldn't tell me much more than that.

Stewart did say that one campaign Aidan and John both worked on was the print ads for Chocolette, which just used the image of a partly unwrapped chocolate bar and the slogan, "Chocolette. So good it doesn't need to be advertised." Stewart told me that the campaign won some national award that year, and I saw the ads in magazines but never learned what award.

Stewart wasn't even sure that John and/or Aidan were gay, or even if it was a gay thing, and he asked me to stop asking him about it.

Conjecture: Stewart knows more of the story than he is willing to share.

Another slogan Aidan produced soon after arriving was the tag for both TV and print ads for Selsa, a new model of luxury car. The text read: "The Selsa CL30. Not first in its class because it's in a class all its own."

Stewart told me that "copyeditor" didn't accurately describe John's job and that John's work relationship to Creative was also hard to describe.

Conjecture: John worked in Creative with Aidan, or else he wasn't a copyeditor at all, if such a job exists at an ad agency.

Conjecture: Stewart doctored the story to make it easier to tell.

Smoking was formally discouraged, but nearly everyone at Gordon/Whackey smoked, and they took smoking breaks in small groups in a kind of informal rotation throughout the day. You had to be at least twenty feet from any G/W entrance to light up, which usually meant the remote parking lot, unless you wanted to stand on Brand Boulevard in the shadow of the building and watch the traffic.

Stewart asked me why I wanted to know so much and why I was so insistent.

Stewart never described how exactly an ad agency works or how he knows what he knows.

After we became friendly acquaintances in school, I didn't see much of Stewart when he moved first to Chicago and then to Los Angeles for work and I stayed in Milwaukee. Most of my communication with Stewart after graduation was limited to email and Facebook messages, which were sometimes infrequent.

Conjecture: There is no Aidan, and it was Stewart with whom John had an intense relationship.

When Stewart asked me why I wanted to know more, I responded that he was the one to share most but not all of the story to begin with. He made it seem important, so it became important, though of course I was only curious because of the mystery of it.

Aidan looks a lot like Stewart looks.

Stewart never told me his exact position at Gordon/ Whackey, but given that we both went to school for graphic design, I just assumed that's what he's doing. That's what I'm doing.

People don't really just disappear of their own accord, do they? They quit work, maybe, and move, or even do something violent, even suicide, but they don't just disappear. If they do, how long does it take before they're officially a missing person? How long before they're found, on average?

Stewart said John was the kind of person who would just quit without telling anyone, and I asked him what he meant, and he told me he couldn't explain it. He could describe John and his appearance and his actions, but not his reasoning, he told me.

Conjecture: Some element of the story is embarrassing to Stewart, preventing him from telling me the entire story of what happened between John and Aidan.

Is it Aidan or should it be "Aidan"?

Aidan, per Stewart, is tall, young, dark-haired, and olive-skinned and always has an easy half-smile on his face. He is charming without being too outgoing, and multiple people of both sexes have been interested in getting to know more about him since he started working in Creative.

Soon after they met, John and Aidan were seen leaving the office together and, sometimes, arriving together in the morning. Several employees thought they spotted the pair holding hands in the parking lot once, while they were both out smoking, but the view was distant.

Why do I need more information than I already have? What do I need to know?

Stewart demanded to know, when I did hear from him, which was more and more infrequently, why I was so interested. It was a simple story—someone disappeared from the office where Stewart worked, and the story spread around and was office gossip for weeks, so Stewart decided he'd share the intrigue and said he never thought I'd get so caught up in it, 1,800 miles away, not knowing any of the people involved.

Stewart said he merely observed and wasn't involved at all, too busy with his own work.

John (if he exists) and I share some features, and if it weren't for the conservative atmosphere here at Clausen, we would dress alike, too, probably.

Nobody disappeared from Clausen International. Once you landed a job, you didn't fish much for other jobs because the stability, benefits, etc., were so great. Living in Milwaukee sucks, but it's workable.

I told Stewart, just tell me everything you remember. Don't hold anything back.

What if John wanted Aidan the way I wanted Stewart?

After John disappeared, his workspace was disheveled-looking, as if he had knocked things over and shook the desk, as if he had somehow struggled or was angry for some reason.

John's workspace was ordinarily very neat. Stewart never described what it looked like, other than that it was very neat. Stewart's details were scarce and selective, but when he provided them, they were vivid.

Once Stewart watched John walk back from Creative to his workspace, smiling wide, his tie loose, taking longer than usual strides, not out of rush but out of confidence.

If John existed.

Conjecture: Stewart made the story up to have something to tell me because we were running out of things to say to each other but still wanted to stay in touch.

At Clausen I don't work on ads but help manage the visual identity of the company, mostly internally but sometimes with external visuals, like the redesign of the corporate logo, which I did not create but which I fine-tuned and produced.

My job is not as interesting as Stewart's. Use of the Internet here is theoretically under watch but in practice is not.

Gordon/Whackey's website uses a lot of Flash with fields of translucent color sliding over each other and has a list of accomplishments, a list of clients, and standard contact information but not much else.

I asked Stewart to try to provide me with an employee roster that predated John's disappearance, but he never responded to that. I asked Stewart to tell me John's last name too, and he responded, *guess*. I asked Stewart if there were any jobs open at Gordon/Whackey, and he told me I wouldn't like it there.

John's last day at Gordon/Whackey was a Thursday, September 21. He was observed (by Stewart?) out smoking with Aidan, but instead of talking they were arguing, John gesticulating wildly. John was quiet the rest of the day after he returned to his work area, and the day after that he was gone forever, though no one knew that yet.

People asked Aidan if he knew what happened to John, but Aidan told them he didn't know John all that well and couldn't say. This was an eyebrow-raiser because a lot of employees had seen John and Aidan together, not just leaving or arriving, but timing their smoking breaks and going out for lunch together. Aidan told everyone that John was a nice guy but that their closeness was exaggerated.

When I asked Stewart for his personal conjecture on the nature of John and Aidan's relationship, he never responded.

When I asked Stewart how his own life was going, he said it was going well, that he had moved up in responsibility enough to afford a decent apartment in Silver Lake and was living with his new girlfriend, Eva, who was a costume designer at Warner Brothers, and they were getting along great, better than he had ever gotten along with a girlfriend.

During school and throughout all our previous correspondence, Stewart never mentioned anything about any girlfriend at all. Everyone at school assumed Stewart was gay.

Conjecture: Eva is a fabrication.

I congratulated Stewart on his new relationship and the new place and asked for pictures, and he sent me pictures that included a woman who could be Eva, but she and Stewart were never in a picture together, and all the pictures of her were taken at a different location than pictures of Stewart (still good-looking) and his new place. The woman in the pictures is always wearing big, dark sunglasses and a flattering blue, floral-print A-line dress. Compared to Stewart's olive complexion, she looks pale. It's hard to read her expression because of the small photo size and the sunglasses, but she's only barely smiling, as if uncomfortable.

Conjecture: John is a fabrication. This could be proven by the fact that Stewart shares only a sloppy collection of facts and seems unconcerned by his disappearance, even as a coworker who didn't know him that well. If someone in Creative here at Clausen disappeared, even Ted, it would still concern me.

If Stewart fabricated John, why would he fabricate his disappearance? Is the disappearance the reason John existed? How was I supposed to respond, other than with natural curiosity? Was I too enthusiastic in my response?

After John vanished, Aidan carried on as usual as if nothing much had happened, and some fellow employees said he was a little more reserved and a little tired-looking; this was debated by Creative when Aidan wasn't around.

Why is Stewart still in touch with me?

Is Stewart still in touch with me?

Yesterday I booked my flight. I'll be in Los Angeles in two weeks. Will Stewart be surprised when he sees me? What do I think he's going to say?

I don't know whether to go to Gordon/Whackey or to Stewart's apartment. Or I don't go to either. Or I go to both?

As long as I'm there in town anyway, I insist?

What does it mean that he shared the story of John's disappearance and certain seemingly random details but wouldn't answer any questions about it?

Conjecture: Stewart is toying with me. Or was.

Conjecture: I have gotten too caught up in John and Aidan because the story sounds exciting—an intense relationship followed by a complete disappearance—and my own life is comfortable now but tedious.

Stewart knows my life is tedious. That's not conjecture at all.

Stewart told me what his address was when I said I wanted to see it on Google Earth. Does Stewart know my plans?

I've told Stewart an awful lot of things.

Is the story of John and Aidan completely true, partly true, or completely fabricated?

Did John vanish on purpose, or was he kidnapped or murdered?

What am I going to say to Stewart when I see him? Say or ask?

On John's last day at Gordon/Whackey, his shirt was untucked, and his tie was loose, and he took a lot of solo smoking breaks after his argument with Aidan, but no one read anything into it until after he was officially gone. John had no close friends at G/W except for, possibly, Aidan.

Could any of this really be true?

Should I knock on Stewart's door? Is the address I have really the right address?

Will Stewart be surprised when he sees me?

Should I use the key under the pot of basil on the porch and let myself in?

Could any of the stories here (including mine), true or not, still have happy endings?

Depending on the story, what would a happy ending be?

SOMEWHERE ELSE ENTIRELY

1.

Or so maybe Kristy nurses her multiple-source and multiple-nature aches and doesn't go to the wedding, maybe she hunkers down in the motel room and sweats things out, twitching minus any external movement, or wanders off into the woods instead. Nothing cataclysmic, nothing chemical, definitely nothing memorable, just a different kind of lingering. A new way to use up too-ample away time. Time away from the usual sucker punch of the day-to-day.

Maybe she leaves her dress on, but maybe she changes

back into her regular outfit of jeans and a plain dark-hued sweatshirt. She's half-in and half-out of the dress now, a teal thing cut low enough to garner attention without being so forward that people will say that she's trying to make everything about her, because as she hunkers she's sure this time it's not about her, nor ever really was. It's somebody else's big day; Kristy is just here, buzzing slightly but not buzzed, and she admires the way her feet look in the white shoes she bought, but she doesn't like how uncomfortable the shoes are and humphs at how wearing her Chuck Taylors with her sundress/sweater combo would not be the appropriate kind of unconventional. She would draw attention to herself again, wrong place, wrong time, and maybe that's the last thing that Kristy Leamer wants to do right now. No need to stick yet more needles into a voodoo doll painted with her own likeness, most clustered at the tender skull. (Maybe she also knows you're not supposed to mix alcohol with benzodiazepines, but desperate times lead and so forth, and maybe Kristy can *feel* the premature wrinkles form on her pale face from landfills full of desperate times.)

So maybe she really could just hunker glossy and half-dressed in the motel room lit by dim, flat daylight and maybe finish her gin and tonic and start another. She has already had one-and-a-half gin and tonics this morning, maybe 60/40 gin/tonic, and she is literally half-dressed and staring down at herself as if she's found something in one of her kitchen junk drawers that doesn't belong to her and that she's never seen before, something that came into her possession unknown. Yet another thing she

doesn't recall stealing. Sitting sloppy and glossy and buzzing and in possession of the foreign her that she really is
and literally half-dressed: she's only even got one earring
in (the left one); the other is sitting by the pearl-colored,
plastic 1980s motel version of a hook-earpiece, curly-cord
push-button landline on the blond (like Rebecca is blond)
wood-grain table between the two double beds. Maybe
she takes out the other earring and tosses it over her left
shoulder for good luck, then plays with the twin lamps
above the bedside table to try to see if one is brighter than
the other.

Or so maybe Kristy just runs—not internally, slam-
ming mental oak doors behind her—but literally, running
out into the parking lot and protesting the vicissitudes
of fate or running wild in the streets as if on fire again,
or not running but jumping sloppily from double bed to
double bed singing "Let's Get Together" from *The Par-
ent Trap* loud and mostly in tune in a chemically scratchy
voice. Or maybe she lies perfectly still on the unmade bed
clutching a white rose, waiting for her prince to come res-
cue her, and maybe her prince is a pleasant, icy insurance
salesman, or maybe her prince is the lead singer of her favorite rock band, or maybe her prince is her friend Rebecca, or maybe her prince is a Mexican bull dyke in yellow flannel who kissed her at a bar once and told Kristy
she called herself Caramel because, she said, she was
"sweet but hard to handle." Maybe several of these things
happen at once. Maybe Kristy watches herself get sucked
into a black hole.

Or maybe Kristy Leamer just sits like this for a long

time, watching dust caught in a slant of sunlight and turning various rocks over in her head. Maybe she lips through her congratulations forward and backward, word by word. Maybe even though she's driven six hours to get here and splurged on a motel room and everything, maybe she doesn't go to the wedding. Maybe she fakes sick again, something exotic like black lung; it doesn't need to be believable, just dire. Maybe she actually takes sick for real, this time, is sick as has been explained to her like instructions, or if not sick then drunk like last night, or if not drunk then toxic as has been explained to her as a warning; maybe she takes to her bed and curls up under motel bed covers and bites an acrylic white thumbnail, or rehearses self-asphyxiation via bedsheet, or mumbles a half-remembered affirmation from the therapist two therapists ago, who implied feeling OK was a kind of form you could just fill out, and lets her eyelids sink, breaking a few mental windows to let herself in somewhere she could spread out and enjoy some natural light.

Or would that just be more or less the same thing as actually going, Kristy thinks, one thing the same as the next, being here or there ending up with the same twisted gut and different kinds of empty bottles and cups, as she slouches into a cringe and kicks off her left shoe. Maybe that's what everyone in her sewing circle would expect. Maybe what people secretly want from Kristy Leamer is a kind of happy ending consisting of her completely going up in wispy gray smoke, a disappearing act, a black hole, a final failure evident in her palpable absence and these certain traces of hesitation: a crinkled but unused

Google Earth map of how to get to the church, a crinkled but maybe-used Google Earth map of how to get to the twenty-four-hour Walmart, assorted mostly unused wedding-attendee paraphernalia (i.e., lipstick, a small, tasteful, unshiny refrigerator-white plastic sequin clutch purse, a mostly empty bottle of chalky "extra" Klonopin), and her clothes in loose heaps and everything wrinkled and looking sour in gauzy daylight. Or maybe she should just show up and be there in order to be there, be a person, a participant, offer up a fixed thin-lip smile, back pew ass-park, and early exit. Because you can dry-swallow Klonopin when you're in the back row, Kristy knows from always being in the back row and having taught herself to dry swallow after Aaron said the flask she used to carry was "a little much, even for you," even when it was just warm, flat Coke minus the fun of rum.

Or maybe she does neither, resists all manner of tugs. Maybe she shakes her head back and forth fast and emits a low moan like a whale beached in a candle factory, wordless discontent surrounded by dim, pretty-smelling tin-roof industry. Maybe sometimes Kristy feels as if her efforts to try to figure out what other people are going to think about her amount to trying to force a key to work in her front door and then realizing that it's the wrong key. Maybe Kristy is more familiar with this feeling than her supply of counselors says is healthy. Maybe this is one of those times, and maybe Kristy kicks off the other shoe and watches it sail in a low arc across a few feet of brown, bulk-bought carpeting. Barefoot, sucking her right thumb, and in command.

And, again: this place is surrounded by woods and wilderness and wildness and not just weddings, and wildness is the morning's menu after last night's pointed fingers and raised voices. The plain wildness of a dead cell phone and streets that lead in a grid of anywhere and everywhere, somewhere more friendly, somewhere else entirely. And the wedding is the wedding of her friend Rebecca, a friend for whom she once had certain feelings she never named, much less expressed, but Rebecca and all her other friends are all getting married sooner or later, the ordinary, normal thing to do, the contractual obligations of being an edges-sawn-off American adult, so skipping one or more actual services isn't going to matter much in the large scheme, because once you've been to one, and so on. And Kristy has parked it in the back pew plenty. Maybe Kristy thinks and even all but just says it out loud to herself: do something new and possibly exciting for a change. Don't go to the wedding and see Rebecca in her chaste gown against her perfect slight tan, but don't make noise about avoiding it either. All things almost being equal, do anything but just keep sitting still, treading water, staring at the black hole, burning out from the inside.

2.

Take a turn two stoplights past the motel room where the wedding attendees are gathering, and you have the edge of the town, already. Or more specifically, you have the twenty-four-hour Walmart that marks the interstate-adjacent remote commerce hub of the small town where

Rebecca is scheduled to get formally married and everything at 1:30 in the afternoon to a nice insurance salesman named Robert on a mostly cloudy late-September Saturday. This is the part of the state that's heavily tree-laden, so off in the distance, once you're standing in the Walmart parking lot, you can see evergreens everywhere, both the spruce and pine varieties that grow in this area. It's not too far northwest, so there are still clear patches that would qualify as meadows if they were more interesting, but mostly the fields just seem like overflow parking lots for trucks or snowmobiles and emphasize how heavily forested this part of the world is anyway.

When you enter the Walmart, you're going to want to head about ten degrees to the right of straight ahead, passing big loads of tube socks and plastic crates and cheap pillows as you head back toward the far wall, where, once you're back there, you have the choice of either what's in front of you (the store's Media Center), what's to the left (men's clothing and shoes), and what you want, which is to the right about fifteen or sixteen aisles, because this is a larger-than-average Walmart. You're going to want to be heading to the right, past the discount home furnishings (on your right) and miscellaneous kids' stuff (on your left), until you get nearly to the back right corner of the store where they keep the Airsoft paintball guns and real guns, but not quite that far. Stop so that the right wall of the store is maybe fifty feet in front of you, and on your left will be the fitness stuff: yoga mats, free weights, etc. You're actually closer than you think, now, because all you have to do is head down that aisle to the small aisle parallel to the left-right one you were just on and wander left for a few more aisles, absentmindedly touching the light gray metal shelving on your right as you go.

So, soon enough you get to the hunting/outdoors area of the store, and you've been in nearly identical Walmarts before so you know where you are with respect to why it is you decided to stop in here on something amounting to a whim. One more aisle and you're in the camping section, tents to the left of you like pricey adult versions of kids' funtime polyethylene domes in bright tent colors (mostly shades of yellow and red), but you want to turn right to where the supplies are. Halfway down the wall is stuff you need if you're going to be headed out into the woods nearby or elsewhere, and so here's where you need to linger, a few dollars folded in one hand, and with the other reach up a little and grab hold of a small ax. A hatchet. When you turn it over in your hand, over and over, to find the answer of what you need it for, you notice how the act of turning it over sometimes bounces the above-head fluorescents off the flat side of the dull hatchet, and it's heavier than you thought, and you're a little surprised at how you arrived at all this so quickly, and you don't even know where you're headed next yet, but the weight of the hatchet is somehow deeply soothing, and for the moment that's enough.

3.

The night before, Scott calls Kristy room-to-room at the motel and not on his cell phone to see if she has plans other than kind of relaxing and maybe watching the marathon of *What Not to Wear*. Kristy picks up the receiver and says she isn't sure, hesitates, says what do you have in mind. Scott was maybe crossing his fingers for *What Not to Wear* so he clears his throat and says something like, oh you know we were all going to get together in somebody's room, but it's definitely not mandatory, it's not some kind of scheduled activity, and this is just FYI. Kristy huffs and sniffs and says, OK, so. Scott says of course the reason he's calling is to see whether she wants to come but you know. You know, he says. What, says Kristy, her voice husky from being buzzed and glossy from buzzing, a little low and a little fast and a little loose with certain consonants. Scott says, oh well you know how it is when we all get together and pound a few, and things being as they are, things are fine, but you know how it is when people are people, and things are totally fine with you as long as there isn't a repeat of what happened last time. You know.

Kristy says, uh-huh, and then she says, what room, and then she hangs up, and then she gets up and stands there rubbing her belly in an absentminded circle and looking out the darkening window, silently trying to rearrange the stuff that is going on inside her. Or maybe after all it's just another case of pay no mind.

BLACK METALLIC

Asshole says he wants to marry me. Again. Say *hell no* to that. Already married three times and him four and I'm exhausted from the whole ordeal. Ask him wherefore he thinks he gets off wanting more marriage. Practice, he says those other marriages were. As if. I sniff at his guff. He says it again, he says, *let's get hitched*, like he's a truck and I'm a trailer. *Fuck* no, I say. We been through this before too. Every spring he gets it together enough to want to make it up to the world for all the screw-ups he's scattered around in the forms of ex-wives and children and lost jobs or Missing Work Time, and he gets up the nerve and buys rings and gets down on his prover-

bial knee and pops the question. I try to say it in bold: I
don't want to get married. Been married and nothing to
it that makes me want to go back there again. There is
nothing left there, with marriage, I say to him, and he just
blinks, stands, says, but I already got the rings. And he
does, though this year he's smarter and he's got the same
rings as last year, he just stored them away for a while. I
still say no. The rings are nothing to look at. Small silver
bands with nothing on them in the way of Promise or Per-
manence. Can't even pick out a decent ring, and why does
he need two, for an engagement? Says he wants to enter
fully into the sacrosanct pact of wedded bliss and I tell
him to take out back and shoot the church talk, this ain't
church and he's five beers gone (never could hold his liquor) and getting glassy-eyed like one of those ugly children in those paintings. Says he won't take no for an answer. I say something to the effect of there's no *negotiating*
going on here, this ain't a strike where we have to enter
into contractual such-and-such, and a no's a no and I got
my own shit to take care of and that's that. He's all glassy-
eyed. I sniff again and sip my Bud. He actually now at this
point gets down off the booth bench and gets back down
on a knee and pleads, and people are looking, and it's not
my idea of how to kill time. Asshole thinks he can win
me over by being demonstrative. My first husband was
demonstrative and he ended up borrowing all my money
and buying that goddamn boat and snaring someone
younger and prettier than me with his used schooner and
his fucking charm. After that, no more demonstrative-
ness. I like my marriages cold and dry, I say, like toast,

no bother, and anyway I'm not on the market anymore and he can just stop, but he stays down there, getting probably a stain on his new Wranglers, and says, c'mon baby now please. I sit and am impassive. I been through this before. He thinks we would make a good match. He thinks we would be great for one another. He thinks we are a match made in heaven, star-crossed lovers, crossed by my own ignorance to our mutual overwhelming rapturous love. Asshole stays down there for a few minutes until he slinks back into the bench booth, brushing off a knee. All mopey. Says that I'm missing out on a great opportunity, that things, such as they are, would be so much better if only. I am unmoved. Asshole then goes for the melodrama, says that if I don't say yes he'll do something self-injurious. Like as if. And anyway what would I care? Says he'll go down to the machine shop where he works and cut his hand off, his ring-bearing hand, just to spite me. He always says stuff like this. Last time it was he was going to jump off Cooper Bridge into the shallow crick and break his neck. I told him, go on ahead and let's see you go on and do it, and that's what I say now. He says, imagine me handless. I say I can imagine that fine. He says, what if both hands. I say why not. He says he'll go on ahead and do it, and it'll be on me. I snort at this, because as if. If a drunken fool sticks his hand too close to a rotary blade of some kind and doesn't have the sense to pull back at the first bloodspurt and/or sign of pain, actually goes through with it, the asshole, what kind of devotion is that? The undying kind, he says. I say he's sick in the head. (I say this a lot, it gets to where I get tired of saying it so much.) He says he'll do it for sure, just wait and watch him, he'll end up with those smooth stumps you see on the amputees on TV and then I'll be sorry because there won't be no rings then. He'll pitch them in the crick, is what he says he'll do. I ask how he's going to do this with no hands, like what, spit them out? Nudge them toward the embankment with his feet? And anyway he's a fool because everybody knows they reattach hands, they can do that kind of stuff now, surgical procedures and such. He says no, he says the wounds would be so bad that it'd be impossible. I sniff again and sip my beer. He says he'd put his hands through the wood chipper out in his back lot, and I ask again how he'll do this handless, but there's no arguing with a drunk and he says they'll be gone, poof, vanished from this earth. I say, well then go ahead and do it. He says he will. I say go ahead. He sits there and stares at me like a depressed puppy. I say they would give him robot hands and he'd be back here henceforth with metal contraptions at the ends of his wrists and be on his knees wrecking his Wranglers again just like always. Because a handless fool is still a fool. He says no, he says his insurance don't cover no *robot hands*, why am I talking crazy, he'll have to settle for those hook things like pirates and old Jeff from the post office have. I say people (Jeff besides) don't wear big hooks on their romantic stumps and he says, sure they do, just ask around. I say he won't be wearing any rings then. He says, well that's the point of it. Lifelong ringlessness. Because of my wanton neglect of his real and true feelings. I reemphasize my lack of care. I briefly picture silver rings slid around the hook hands, and the image of it, with the rings able to be spun around the hook at the whim of the handless, is funny and also bleak. But not because Asshole is involved. It's just a bleak image, is all. He says next morning if I don't give him a little bit of hope he's going to go ahead and get the hook hands, and everybody will go on about calling him Hook Boy and he'll acquire the hushed pity of the whole town. I stare at my beer. He says I'll live to regret it, and I say it's his hands, he can do what he wants with them, and he says he'll still be sexy and girls local and otherwise will be attracted because of the danger. I almost spit up my swig of beer at this. He says he can't wait to see it, how I'll come around, and we won't be able to make human natural love because of the hook hands. But, he says, he bets me a crisp twenty that he can still unhook my bra with hook hands, even. I say the bet is on, and then I kiss the asshole, and we kiss again over the booth table, sloppier, and then I send him on his way.

FORMERS (AN INDEX)

ALLEN, DOUGLAS. Like sucking a lemon. A frozen one. That was conversation with him. Not at first but fast, lightning quick from easy grin to let's not and say we did. And not much to stare back at. Never anything in bed and seldom in bed, him always at work talking, when he did talk, him talking numbers and schedules and rules. It was brief, it cooled off quick, cold as a frozen lemon, only a few months I think, him now in a refrigerator downtown somewhere, brick-silent, thinking complicated math.

BAKER, WILLIAM. The escort. Drove me when I needed the MRI. Insisted. Called it companionship. That's what it was, start to stop, no tidal wave or aching thirst, just constant hum coming from another room. He cared. He did his best to care as hard as possible. He didn't know what to do, so eventually we shook hands, literally, we literally just shook hands like it was a transaction ended, the whole deal done. William Baker who got to see the CD stills of what my brain looks like. Cloudy slices of organic-looking puff with maybe here or there a dark spot.

BRADLEY, STONE. Real first name. And this already makes it look like it's only tight white guys. Straight white guys. Not always. The main things about him were that he wasn't all that different from everybody else, and he shrugged at what we were, and he had a broken-bent nose acquired he never said how. Not sure I ever asked.

CALDWELL, HECTOR. Like silver and violet sky, everywhere, electric, only electric while it lasted, wide as the sky too, the feeling, being near him, with him, him a lightning rod. A lightning field. A furtive man with expert hands. That was when I first started blossoming symptoms, my own electrical storms. A faraway man expert at looking elsewhere. Over his shoulder. At least he went all the way, cheating on me with not one but three random men. He packed quickly and apologized succinctly because he was nonetheless nice.

DANLEIGH, ROBERT. The operatic one. Constantly hitting a high C—in bed, at the restaurant, on the phone explaining to me how things were, that there was a distance, and it was between us, and it was growing. He said I was too preoccupied with myself and couldn't get out of my own head. I was busy covering my ears.

ELLIS, JOHN. Too much like me for me to find much to work with.

GARCIA, FRANK. Afraid of silence. Afraid of me, of my illness, of what to do with ourselves when not careening 90 mph. Afraid of himself, probably. Afraid of what he could and couldn't do. Brief because you need silence as much as you need a body in your bed that isn't yours.

GROBEL, PHILLIP. A companion like Baker but chronologically prior. A hand-holder. Sharp and crisp and always somehow far away. I was sick then, shouldn't have been involved at all, but he was utilitarian, made being there his gift to me, even as he sat in the waiting room as far away as the sunset in the hospital's pushily bland framed print. Never could gather enough of a hand for him to hold so he shook loose, let go, drifted far away into the sunset, maybe.

HAAS, STANLEY. Followed me from the bedroom to the ambulance, followed the ambulance to the ER, followed me everywhere, followed me home like a professional stray. Turned his head and looked into you like one. When he ran out of (external and internal) places to follow me when I got tired and stood still, he followed someone else, fierce in elsewhere pursuit, but even then a trail of breadcrumbs back.

KENWORTH, DUNCAN. Funereally removed and quiet. May as well have been dead. Well-dressed, though. Clean and smelling of something you wished you could touch.

LEE, THOMAS. Different with him, deeper, more complicated. Like more than one part of the engine malfunctioning at once, a slurred stump speech that promised mutual gifts, mutual kisses, mutual resentment when we weren't everything the other wanted to hook and pull. But different. An understander. He listened in and most of the time followed along. Start and stop by mutual agreement, let's be friends later, let's not be intense, let's not linger or stare, let's pretend we're going to call each other after it ends.

LUTTER, JACOB. Passed through almost like a ghost in a room so full of ghosts he could barely make it door to door. The time span on him was tight, what with some other ghosts already in my head, but him never around long enough to ever even really have arrived.

MICHELSON, MICHAEL. Too much noise in the love-you-too signal. A nine-month sore spot. A whole ocean in his eyes but not yours for wading into, rocks in your pockets.

MOREL, STEPHEN. For bedroom purposes only. No spark despite all the friction. Me still mystery-sick, still searching the faces of doctors looking at me head-tilted. Never told him what I was maybe sick with; never got around to buying a get-well-soon card for him to give to me.

MUCLANSON, GEORGE. Too much George in him, not enough forward thrust.

MULLINS, ALEXANDER. When I got sick, I settled into it and loosened the leash of mate-need constantly pulling me forward. He came through and knew me, was an examiner, details and craftsmanship, knew exactly how to fix my hair when I was too sick with sick. Took care of me and floated love like hovercraft, ridiculous but tempting, knew that he had to leave when there was no more care to take. Wanted to be there but missed by a few inches. I was too sick with sick to snap him into place. One you wanted to know more about, past and present, but no hotline to dial for that, no details in the mostly unused files.

NG, ALAN. Contact sports a good few years before either of us knew what we were doing. Before I got sick and got honest. We wandered around in the dark of each other. We tossed coins into mental fountains, got nowhere, bred misunderstanding, got glassy-eyed and kicked each other out for no good reason other than young frustration like a cloud that wouldn't lift. Still get postcards from him in the form of late-night phone calls full of garbled wish.

OCTAVO, LOREN. A lover and a fighter. More fighter than lover. Mostly the fights were more memorable and interesting with you getting front seat for getting your delicate feelings thrown across the room. He knocked everything over in me, but I needed an excuse to redecorate that wasn't hermetic sulk and got it out of him when he was there and a while afterward. Blue-eyed and whisker slim, and acted like both were historically important.

PEARSON, GEORGE. A brief encounter at the nadir. He was there too with a bottle to hug, no arms to hold me. Only necessary flesh to press against. Flawless downstairs though, and a sculpted facade before he stopped sculpting. The ugly midnight before I got figured out.

RAKKAE, HNOR. The one who assumed he could fix me, fast and on a budget, just through distraction. Simplistic pleasures. Best part was his slow-motion smoke-puff disappearing act.

RALK, CHRISTOPHER. Careful. Not cautious but deliberate. The one you label in your inventory as the one that got away. Careful with his smile, his humor, his constant even-pressure gentleness, a gentleman, careful with his love and only unwrapping it in private. It was enough to live on. He was enough of something to hold onto. He was something. He held instead of pulled, pushed instead of shoved. He wanted to be there, and, odds were, he was. Careful not to get hurt, careful not to showcase his acid anger, careful. And then we got reckless and things tore loose and I got lost in what could have been, and that was before I even got sick, months before the storm that followed me around, the fog that came and clouded other, lesser men.

SABELBERG, JOSHUA. The card-carrying lost cause. Not worth the janitorial bother. Good in bed but grim when fully dressed. Even scrambled eggs or mixed drinks got solemn, soon tiresome, a murky shallow pool you don't think you should probably get your feet wet in.

STEVENS, EDWARD. Wordless, borderless fucking, constant and for approximately forever, and it was almost enough.

TALENDER, HALWELL. Nothing at the other end of that line and that was fun, but being sick took time and focus and getting well took more, and he was always only face-close, mostly timewaster, a game I didn't want to play because it was too easy, because I mastered it too quick.

TRENT, SAL. Flimsy faith healer. Bad with his hands and his news.

WILLIAMS, FELLOW. All he ever did was insist. Which was everything I ever wanted when I was sick, at least for a handful of thin winter months. I admired, when I pushed him away, how fast and far he slid. Maybe still out there, staring out windows, hands in his lap, ready to begin.

WITHIN REASON

Come over here, he said, and I did, and he said, tell me everything about yourself, and I did, and I said to him, tell me everything about yourself, and he did, within reason, he said, and you're very attractive, he said, and I said, likewise, and he said, is this the part where we kiss, and I said I didn't know, and he said, why don't we find out, and so we did, and do you think anyone was watching, he said, and I said I didn't know, and he said, what do you do in bed, and I said, I'll do a lot of things, and I said, what do you do in bed, and he said, it depends upon the circumstances but I'll do anything, within reason, he said, and you smell good, he said, and I said, likewise, and he said, let's kiss again, and I said, let's find somewhere more private, and so we did, and we locked the door behind us, but there was no bed, which was OK, he said, because who needed a bed, and he took a pair of handcuffs out of his pocket and dangled them in front of me, and I said, what are you planning to do, and he said, guess, and I said that he planned to put the handcuffs on me, and he said I was right, and he did, my hands cuffed behind my back, and I said, I don't usually do this kind of thing, and he said, what kind of things do you usually do, and he kissed me, his hands on the sides of my head, and I kissed back, and then I said I could do anything, within reason, and he said that it was a little late for second guessing, and I said, that's not what I meant, and he unbuttoned my shirt and pulled it back so it hung from my arms behind me, and he said, you're beautiful, and I said, so are you, and then he sat in a chair for a while, looking at me, and I stood there, looking back at him, and then I said, what are you thinking about, and he said, I was thinking about you, and I said, what about me, and he said, are you excited by the unexpected, and I said, I usually am, and he left the room and closed the door behind him, and I waited for a long time, thinking about where he could be, and then I decided to sit down in the chair where he had sat, and I waited for him to return, and I had a hard-on on and off, and I wondered whether we were playing a game, and if so who was winning, and I wondered whether something had happened to him, and I wondered whether what he had told me about himself was true, and I wondered where he got the handcuffs and why he carried them with him, and I decided to stand back up, and I paced, and I started to get cold, and I waited for a long time, and I wondered whether I should try to open the door and go search for him, or for anyone, and didn't know whether I should, and when the people who came in and found me there asked me what I was doing like that, I had to say I wasn't really sure.

ESCAPOLOGY

The extra soft-box short-life tungsten fill light the crew brought is making the officers a little skittish, even though it's really ultimately the precinct's fault (as much as *fault* could be assigned) that the police station nearest Channel Five's headquarters was so dingy. The place looked particularly televisually dirty on account of the beige brick walls' sickliness under the neat rows of fluorescents and the reflections of disorganized desks and files and chairs in all of the interior subdivisional office windows of the precinct—this being an inner room in the building, there weren't any windows to the outside world (which was sunny and unusually warm for early spring), just the kind of windows that opened onto the walls of other rooms. The whole place had a cavernous feel that necessitated the fill light. Under it, the officers cast soft-edged shadows on their workplace, industrial desks topped with dusty or crowded inbox/outbox trays and brown stuffed accordion files and stacks of paperwork and a muted rainbow of weather-beaten-looking binders and here and there a pencil-holder mug with a badge emblazoned on it, surrounded by uncomfortable-looking tan office chairs at odd rotations and uniformly gray cylindrical trash cans and loose piles of both hard and soft cop-related effluvium, and a dry erase board in the back on which the only thing written was the word "effectiveness" in black all caps, as they stood around in the background waiting for the filming of the remote to be over with (since the whole mess was embarrassing enough). The lights lent the atmosphere a kind of magic-show theatricality that the newest and hence lowest-on-the-totem-pole team reporter for Channel Five is trying to shut out of his mind as he turns his back to the camera (having just finished the spiel about how this was all going on according to official police procedure) and looks at his soft shadow as it slightly shades a nearby desk and crumples his face in concentration and curses himself under his breath.

The task at hand is for the unlucky reporter to have his hands cuffed behind his back and then, as quickly as possible, work the cuffs under him so that he stands with his hands cuffed in front. The light is bright enough to make the officer applying the cuffs to the reporter squint a bit and block the shot, which means several tries before they got a good shot of the cuffing of the reporter's hands behind his back with what the officer had assured the reporter on-camera were standard-issue police handcuffs (not the newer kind that hinged, the reporter thought as he bit his lip, but the regular old U.S. kind you see on cop shows). The reporter was a little flustered by the delay, but could finally nod to the nearby officer who was holding a stopwatch to go ahead and start, hoping that, as he turned, the slight bulge in his pants wouldn't cast any kind of noticeable shadow of its own either, to anyone personally in the room or to the viewers at home. As he begins to slip his cuffed hands down behind him over his ass, he hopes his suit pants bulge such that they rumple (this is how it had looked in the mirror during rehearsals, but he didn't want to lose concentration and stare down at his crotch, on TV, thereby drawing attention to it) from the awkward squatting position the reporter is now moving into as a means to help ease his hands down over the rear of his hips to the small of his knees, similar (in theory) to what Greg Johnson had done the previous evening when, after being arrested for grand theft auto, he'd somehow managed to slip his cuffed hands from behind him to in front of him, as his arresting officers drove him in a police wagon to the downtown central station, and thereby grab a service revolver from one of the surprised officers, commandeer the wagon in which he'd been transported, and escape. His whereabouts were (still, at this point) unknown.

This was last night's late-breaking news story and was novel and ratings-spiking, and the stations had all scrambled to cover it only to realize that the nature of the escape was such that there wasn't much to show, other than filed reports from in front of the yellowish halogen-lit downtown jail, which is where people with seniority on the Channel Five news team had first assembled to solemnly report the story, but when there was no subsequent discovery and capture of the escaped Mr. Johnson, the various newsrooms had to scramble for footage to fill up the televisual gap, since this was, of course, TV, and the viewing audience wasn't just going to stay tuned to stare slack-jawed at something that was merely described and not shown. Hence the current remote, the intention of which (the producer told the young reporter when he'd arrived that morning) was to provide some visual illustration of how this sort of thing could have gotten going.

So when the reporter arrived at work that morning, having already had one serious discussion with his boyfriend, and was handed a pair of handcuffs and a stopwatch and was told to get to work, he knew already that there would be trouble. And now with his cuffed hands behind the small of his knees, pausing for a second to steady his balance, he is struck briefly by the thought that his boyfriend might see him on TV, and that even if the general viewing audience wouldn't recognize his erection, that his boyfriend would, a flash-through of thought that actually encourages the erection along and causes the reporter to shift away from the camera slightly, such that now the general viewing audience is left with a better view of his trim, gabardine-trousered ass instead of anything more problematic. He shifts his weight to his right foot and gets his balance before lifting his loafered left foot off the precinct floor in order to start to position his toe through the loop formed by his cuffed hands, which were flushed red with strain, the idea being to poke the toe of his left foot back through the loop and then put his left foot down behind him and shift so that he would now be squatting with his hands cuffed between his legs (near, unfortunately, his crotch), in order to get his balance so as to lift the other foot through. The first serious conversation he'd had with his boyfriend in the morning had concerned how the boyfriend had quit his job at a brokerage firm, which was not quite upsetting but still unpleasant, even though the boyfriend has quite a considerable sum of money stashed away, on account of good investments and a sizable inheritance from a childless rich uncle who nobody else in the boyfriend's family liked but who said he saw himself in the reporter's boyfriend—but money was money. What was troubling and serious about the morning revelation was that this was not the kind of thing the reporter's boyfriend did. The boyfriend, who was longterm, was not an impulsive person and hadn't ever complained either about his work or the people he worked with, so all morning the reporter had found it hard to concentrate on learning how to do what the producer had dubbed the Johnson Maneuver, concerned as he was about his boyfriend's odd behavior and the plausibility of his own televised erection.

The boyfriend in question was the first that had indulged the reporter's proclivities for being tied up in a way that went beyond corny silk scarves or fur-lined handcuffs into the realm of really strict and pleasurably uncomfortable bondage. Last night the reporter had persuaded the boyfriend to gag and blindfold him and tie him face-down, spread-eagle on the bed and leave him like that, even after they'd fucked, while the boyfriend went back downstairs to do the dishes and work for an hour or so on his crane project (he was making a thousand cranes as a gift for a dying friend—nobody that the reporter knew personally), before climbing back up the stairs of their townhouse to fuck the reporter again, this time with his fingers, before untying him so that the reporter could take a shower and go downstairs to watch TV and the boyfriend could go to sleep. There was no indication last night that he'd quit his job, even though the boyfriend had been more reserved than usual and less than enthusiastic (it seemed) about indulging the reporter's proclivities, but then again, the boyfriend had his moods and was worried about his dying friend, so the reporter, the right side of his head pressed to the bed as he listened, motionless, to the clinks of the dishes being washed downstairs, wasn't unduly worried then, but the revelation this morning of the sudden decision was disquieting, not only because it was so sudden, but because they'd had the whole previous evening to discuss it.

In the precinct office, the reporter now has his foot through the loop, and once he slides the leg through past the knee (the cuff of his trousers briefly catching on the metal of the cuffs), he steps back down again, both feet on the tile floor, stopwatch seconds ticking. The producer had laid a bet with a producer at another station about whose luckless reporter could do the trick more quickly, and there was that to be concerned about as well, since the reporter knew that if he lost his producer's bet, he'd end up with more stories like this, ridiculous stunts or feel-good filler—things involving children or animals. The reporter didn't like children or animals either as an assignment or in real life, and that was incentive to hurry up, but he was at the point of almost being finished, and now he'd have to stand upright again, his hands in front of him, the veins in his wrists pulsing, and there was the chance that his erection, lingering in a kind of nether-world short of full tumescence, might be caught in the shot, which would have consequences worse, he thinks, than losing a bet.

The reporter had even gone home at lunch to search for dark pants from his own wardrobe that hid an erection well, which led to the second serious conversation of the day (if you could call it that) with the boyfriend, whom the reporter discovered sitting in the living room, surrounded by several hundred small white paper cranes, crying. Part of the agenda of the reporter's hastily taken lunch was the hope that his boyfriend might help him out, sexual-exhaustion-wise, but there he was instead, weeping, and the reporter didn't know what to say and watched him briefly in the soft afternoon light before asking what was wrong. The boyfriend didn't say anything, but just shook his head. The reporter asked if it was the dying friend, if that was the cause of the sur-prising disconsolation, but the boyfriend simply shook his head *no* and looked away, blowing his nose with a wad of Kleenex as the reporter ran his fingers around the edge of the handcuffs in his jacket pocket, wondering how delicate the situation was and whether there was anything he could say or do, any kind of puzzle he could solve that would reverse the course of his boyfriend's sourness and put everything back on the right track, so that rather than weeping, surrounded by paper cranes and Kleenex, the boyfriend could brusquely cuff the reporter's hands behind his back, threading the chain through one of the kitchen chair's posts before undoing the reporter's fly and jerking him off in the bright kitchen so that later in the day the reporter would be less likely to accidentally scandalize Channel Five's viewing public (which was not big because Channel Five was third in a crowded market, but was still big enough, and the last thing any reporter wanted was to become a story himself, even if just informally among the crowd of on-air personalities that lived in Milwaukee), but the reporter could see that there was no way he could ask this of his weeping boyfriend, especially if he didn't even know why his boyfriend was weeping, even though the reporter desperately needed it, needed it just as badly (he supposed) as whatever it was the boyfriend had lost (internally or otherwise) and couldn't find or fix, and the reporter ended up simply watching his boyfriend cry, leaning against the archway that separated living room from dining room, nudging a crane with his foot for what might have been several minutes before the boyfriend stopped crying but stayed quiet, refusing to explain anything, sitting perfectly still.

In the lit-up station, as he shifts his weight to his left foot and raises his right foot (all this time, still half-squatting, the tip of his tie—a maroon and navy striped deal that was his Wardrobe favorite—occasionally brushing the dusty tile floor), he wonders how many minutes he'd stared at his boyfriend in frustration and concern before the boyfriend had waved him away, saying he was fine, they would talk about it later, maybe, and as the reporter brings his right leg up and backward through the loop, he blushes a bit but is relieved, mostly, to think that his erection is now conveniently fading, thinking, as he stands up to show his cuffed hands to the waiting camera after fourteen seconds of struggle—how earlier that day, after being waved off, instead of pressing the issue, asking the questions he knew the boyfriend wanted to be asked and spending lunch comforting him, he'd instead climbed the stairs alone and closed the bedroom door behind him, took the cuffs out of his jacket pocket and put them on, stood in front of the full-length mirror, and slipped one cuffed hand quietly down his pants.

CLEAN AND FRIENDLY

1.

Sometimes my husband comes home covered in blood. Which is weird on its own, but especially weird because he's a pharmaceutical sales rep. And when we're talking blood, we're not talking *Carrie* buckets of pig blood (at least not yet, I hope). We're talking more flecks, a splatter, sometimes even so fresh that we can get it out of his suit. While he has the money to buy new suits if they get ruined, suit shopping can be a hassle because my husband is tall and thin and off-the-rack stuff never quite fits, too short in the sleeves, and presentation is key, he always says, in his line of work. Sales is sales, and he does look, let's say, very sharp going to work every morning, but then usually around 6 p.m. he gets home, and sometimes there's the blood.

I never ask him, and he never volunteers. There's the fact of it, of course, the incongruity of *why* blood, even when you're around medical staffers all day except when en route, but it's something we don't talk about. My sister Judy thinks I'm crazy not to even raise the question. Perhaps politely, before he leaves in the morning to fetch his rolling suitcase and stock up on freebies at the office before he's out in the field. But part of why my husband and I are so drama-free as a couple is because we don't ask when we don't need to. We let ourselves be separate people, and my sister thinks love is more about, let's say, *enmeshment*.

I did ask him once whether it was his blood, actually the first time it happened, because he looked a little alarmed coming in, a little skittery, but he just shook his head and asked whether we had any stain remover, which we did. It didn't work that time, and it wasn't one of his better suits, so he didn't frown much at the loss—he's not very talkative outside of work—but it's an environmental problem because you can't donate suits to Goodwill if they're splattered, so you just have to toss them. I feel bad about that, but what can you do?

My husband and I met when we were undergrads, both psych majors at Indiana State. We weren't the inseparable kind of head-over-heels lovers, but we were instantly compatible, let's say *confluent*. We married right out of college, and I wanted to get my MD eventually in psych, and he didn't have the inclination for more school, so he picked up the pharmaceutical sales rep job right out of college, and he proved good at it and happy with it and stuck with it all through my schooling. My residency is on hold now at Froedtert Hospital because we just had our first child, Jackson, and taking care of him plus going full-time into residency, which would have been or will be at Columbia Psychotherapy, is just not possible to pull off at the same time right now, so I'm waiting until Jackson is through some crucial stages and I can place him in daycare without too much remorse and get back into it, because I do love what I do. Right now that's just a stay-at-home deal, which I love as much as work but which makes me itch when it comes to the nominally housebound nature of it. So when my husband does come home covered in blood, at least there's something novel to do, though I hope that the amount of blood doesn't increase. And the next question to ask him is whether the blood is human or not, but I'm working up to that.

2.

The constant push is tough. Every day. Every single day. Except weekends and holidays. It's what I call the Shine. Presentation is key. You go in and you have your appointments on your phone and you hit your marks and shine. I don't mean shine as in shiny or as in make your parents proud. I mean presentation. Representation. Presentation is key. The product is the product and you hand it off and it is an extension of your handing it. The constant push is tough. Everything is an extension of you, and you need to be precise, in place, exact. Surgical. Polished shoes. Interesting but not flashy tie. Flattering suits and shirts. White teeth. Smooth skin. Tidy haircut. The constant push is tough. It doesn't matter what you're pushing, as long as you know how to push. Which is not true. All salespeople are presentable, but your product is an extension of you and you are an extension of it, and pharmaceuticals are clean and modest and helpful, so you are clean and modest and helpful. You produce a modest shine and hold it in place all day. All day long. Not in the car driving from mark to mark, but on the mark, in through the compression swoosh of the automatic doors with your roller, you smile easily but not for no reason. You are confident. You want to exhibit your product, you want to convince, you want to push, because you're proud of what modern medicine has done. Everything is on display. The constant push is tough. The drives from mark to mark are different. You are a different person. You practice your Shine and you check your phone but you do not display the Shine. You reserve it. Recommended daily doses. It doesn't matter what kind of pharmaceutical. The Shine is the same. You're a different person at the mark, one-on-one, you lean forward slightly, you construct the impression that you care what the doctor thinks, you present and display. You hand off the goods, and you make sales. You do what you do, and the variations are only in what you are extending and to whom you extend. You are clean and friendly. The constant push is tough. Perfection may not be attainable, but it is still our goal. "Perfection is our goal" is our motto. We have a motto. The company. All of us out in the field. Perfect extensions of the perfect remedy. Clean. Friendly. The goal is perfection. Here or there a little slip. Here or there something happens. So Plan B. New angle of attack. If this doesn't help one person, it will help another. It must. That is what it was made to do. That is why I am here. Extending this to you. This is the Shine, and it is for you to see, it is a bridge from me to you via the product. Clean and friendly. The constant push is tough.

3.

Quiet suburb in a quiet city on a quiet lake. Now and then a storm passes through and the maples' leaves all turn up to the sky, the trees looking folded inside-out. Not much ever happens, which is by design. The local papers feature stories about county jail inmates fighting over watching either *Jeopardy* or the Discovery Channel, or about the city council plan to turn off every other streetlight in order to save electricity costs. Most crime is concentrated in a small mixed-race but mostly African-American C-shape of a neighborhood called Uptown, and there's always news from Uptown, and it's rarely good, except when a church does something or more public art gets installed in the city council's attempt to gentrify it. But mostly this small, quiet city is a place where people from Chicago and Milwaukee come to get away from the thrum of their larger, more complicated cities. The view of the lake is nice, and you can canoe along the slow, low Root River that starts north and empties out downtown. It's a nice place, maybe a little insular, but nowhere you'd want to escape unless you longed for complexity and thrum. Strangers smile at each other in the street, and every year there's an event called the Color Run where spectators flock to a race route to throw colored cornstarch at white-garbed runners, and the best photos of it are always front-page news.

The town is not the kind of place where people leave their doors unlocked, but even as the population slowly dwindles, the citizens try to hold together a sense of the city's long history and homespun charm. Soon after the Color Run, though, active city walkers and bicyclists begin noticing small pools in the streets, and the puddles look red, and not the kind of red from a wet Color Runner. But they always vanish quickly, sometimes even before the police can arrive, and when the police do arrive, they cordon off the scene and lean over and look and take samples, quickly and quietly, not wanting to raise the eyebrows of residents. For a while, there's the unspoken question of whether they're even real, or just dirty water puddles or pavement seen from odd angles. Citizens eventually become concerned, though, because people do see the puddles and people do see the police arriving at them and obscuring them from view, because even though nobody says the word, everyone wonders about whether it's blood and, if it is, where it might have come from.

The hushed investigation continues for several weeks while residents wait, some losing interest, or gaining interest in the fact that the cops take it seriously, rather than in what it actually is. When the police finally are pushed to give a press conference, the chief keeps it brief and says only that their analysts cannot confirm if the pools are or are not what he calls "human fluid," that current results are inconclusive and inconsistent, but that he and his team are hard at work solving the problem and ensuring residents are safe. The story makes headline news in the local paper, but so did the story about when the police department decided to change the color of their uniforms to dark blue. The headline reads "'Human Fluid' Still Unknown," and local residents read it and most just shrug, because after all, it's not even a crime, or evidence of some kind of crime, probably, just some fluid, possibly not even human. Strange things sometimes just happen, even here, and even though the puddles continue to appear and disappear, slowly growing larger in size, life in the small, quiet city goes on.

HAPPY ENDING

The story begins with Lucy feeling lucky re: her former high school burning down because she's cooking a pot roast and she can walk from the kitchen, where the fire is happening on Channel Four on the countertop TV, over to her living room bay window, where she can see it live and in its full, smoky glory. The crux of the matter here is how Lucy feels about living across the street from her former high school, now eight or ten years on after graduation, because her high school years were not under any circumstances The Best Years of Her Life, and so the sight of the massive gray brick building burning out from the inside presents her with a set of questions about her own mixed emotions. Questions such as: How does she feel about the blaze, apparently (according to TV conjecture) the result of an electrical short? Does part of her feel happy? Does part of her also maybe feel sad, as much as sadness is involved here, because after all, here is a major era of young Lucy's life irrevocably destroyed, plus a fire of that magnitude causes probably a lot of environmental damage? Also, maybe, does she feel a certain muted relief, clutching the curtains at her living room window and seeing her pale oval face and slough of thick brown hair reflected against the blaze and fire and news crews by her interior kitchen lights? Or maybe she doesn't really feel anything at all except that her feet hurt and she's hungry and she hates her job, because let's assume that Lucy hates her job not viscerally, like an enemy, but because of the material facts of it: how like a high school it is, how she spends limitless hours there doing things over and over again that are of no interest to her, because basically this is maybe (she is thinking, looking at the fire) what her youth has set her up for. Endless work. A life from which, we're probably supposed to assume, something must be lacking.

This is where the story should flash back to recount What Lucy Was Like in high school, but the truth of the story is that this flashback would not be particularly interesting, because high school for Lucy was just a dull, gray sameness given a certain hormonal arc by puberty, and that's about it. There's no prom story (she didn't go), there's no being-picked-on stories (she wasn't), there's no tender moments between her and her friends that

Changed Everything, because that's not what Lucy's high school experience was actually like. This is not to say that Lucy was a formless, ahistorical lump of a person, but rather that she doesn't view what happened to her in high school, good or bad, as particularly formative in terms of who she is now, making a pot roast.

Her job is another story, though. This is why a narrative flashback to moribund teenagerdom might reveal some conflict re: Lucy being advised by the high school counselor to get on and stay on the Business Track even though she only pulled low Bs and Cs in typing and accounting, etc., or she maybe already knew that work was not where she was going to find meaning in her life, but she, as had her parents before her, had to find a way to pay the bills, especially the health insurance her job doesn't offer and for which she needs to cough up over $500 a month because of pre-existing conditions which probably aren't germane to the story. (The conditions, nonetheless: a slight case of scoliosis, TMJ, generalized anxiety disorder, and body dysmorphic disorder, though Lucy would argue if you cornered her on it that approximately 99 percent of people everywhere suffered from body dysmorphia—they just didn't have to lug around the tag of it and the ridiculousness of knowing that you know that you have distorted perceptions of your own body. Because who doesn't have an odd-angle view of themselves, one way or another?)

And yet: Here's Lucy's high school, burning down. And she was unlucky enough to find the best two-bedroom apartment close to her job in a duplex that just happened to be across the street from where she used to assemble for homeroom every morning for four years. And there's not much to say about the high school burning down because the fire is interior, and according to news reports Lucy half-listens to as she goes back to check her pot roast (those things can dry out fast if you're not careful), the school is burning from the inside out, and even though Lucy has the distance of the faculty parking lot to get a good sight of the south end of the school, mostly all she sees, either on TV or in person, is dark, gray smoke.

Or maybe it would be a good idea to present a day in the life of Lucy then (in high school, going through the motions) vs. Lucy now, going through different motions. And there's the question of what happened in the eight or ten or maybe eleven or twelve years since Lucy graduated, though her college and post-college years consisted of sowing the same kind of wild oats that everybody at her age and in her situation sows, namely drinking a lot, doing a little bit of drugs (pot only), and sleeping around (men and women), until all three started to seem more like work than like the Fun that Lucy sometimes lies in bed on weekends and wonders about. Fun as in: Is she having any? Is Fun in her life, and if it's not, is Fun something she should actively pursue? And if so, how? Life, liberty, and the pursuit of happiness notwithstanding, most of Lucy's experiences of fun, of Fun, seem kind of hollow in retrospect, and so maybe by the end of the story you get the idea she's now more interested in Comfort than Fun. Comfort being deeper and longer-lasting, if you can find and hang onto it.

And re: the job that Lucy currently works: she's an administrative assistant. Mostly she moves around, in various ways, large amounts of information of questionable worth. Since she gave up college during her junior year, she has always been an administrative assistant, and she probably doesn't ever imagine a down-the-road career switch or return to school, unless it's something more personally rewarding and Fun like photography or ceramics, so administrative assisting is where it's at, for Lucy, and there's a whole culture of mining humor from the absurdity of the contemporary workplace, but for Lucy it boils down to seeing to what extent she can get away with checking her email or reading blogs and tumblrs without it being a privilege that has to be taken away from her, as it was at her last job three years ago and which is why she left for a different company. The online world is nothing if not distraction itself; Lucy has friends who read romance novels or thrillers or watch lots of TV, but for Lucy the sheer endlessness of crazy junk (e.g., LOLcats, YouTube, celebrity gossip) is her main source of adult fun, so for Lucy, the Internet is like one long romance novel that never even makes it to the first sex scene, because there's so much interesting and probably useless but fascinating stuff to discover before you get there, stuff that is unexpected, stuff that is not like her actual life, which right now is very much expected, which is neither here nor there, except maybe it's neither Comfort nor Fun.

And it should also be mentioned that everybody who was in the high school at the time of the late-afternoon fire got out safely, so that's not an issue either.

Or instead of the fire approaching something symbolic, with Lucy standing there letting her pot roast dry out as she clutches the curtain and watches an institutional location from her past generate a ton of smoke, it might be a better idea to skip ahead a few years to when Lucy isn't living across from the burnt-down high school at all and has settled down with a decent woman she met at the place she works and now only administrates part time and takes a few classes in photography at her old school, because she and her partner have had a child they named Colin, after the partner's older half-brother, who died young of Hodgkin's. Is Lucy having less Fun now, or more, or should she even be thinking of things in those terms? Is Fun still a worthwhile question? And anyway, what's more troubling now is that Colin, who is three, has an obsession with sources of light, including (and this is the troubling, yet for the purposes of the story, ironic, part) fire, meaning that he's gotten burned a few times here and there in small ways but continues to not be able to separate himself from the light and heat, even though at his age he should know, Lucy thinks, gazing down at him playing trucks on the floor while she sits on the sofa with her laptop. And then Lucy searches in her mind for some sort of pattern that would explain her kid's behavior in terms that were decisive and that could lead to some sort of quantifiable action, but she doesn't come up with anything because she's never had a real personal experience with fire. At this point in the story, then, she remembers that there was that time her former high school burned down while she lived across the street from it, but that wasn't a *pattern*, it was just an unrelated incident that she didn't even mention to her coworkers the next morning, and maybe Lucy forgets about being happy and the wide arc of her life and spends a few moments trying to remember what she was thinking when she watched the fire for a few minutes before she let go of the curtain and went back to dinner (whatever it was), but she just shrugs instead and puts down her laptop and pushes herself down off the sofa in order to play flashlight tag on the living room walls with her beautiful son.

MISADVENTURE

This is not necessarily a proclamation of anything. Though I thought perhaps you should know, being remote and discrete yet knowing all of the main players in the narrative, that is to say, all of us men in the apartment complex on San Vincente Boulevard. My recent correspondence has been full of false cheer and misleading matters, and now is the time to set things right so you have a clear view of what transpired and can apply your own consideration to the matter.

Q. Whom is Martin addressing in his message(s)? Q. How would the recipient know all of the friendly neighbors at the

apartment complex? Q. Why does Martin now feel com-
pelled to report what has "transpired"? Q. What might be
some reasons why his diction is so stilted and formal?

AUGUST

I need to acknowledge both the paucity of my reports and
their brief nature but inform you that much has happened
that has been cumbersome to relay. Things have become
as intricate as they have become tenuous in certain re-
gards concerning all of us, now. I do not wish to delay reporting the matter with Bob. I do not hasten to it either.
It's important to get right to the main line with what happened to Bob.

First, however, I must point out that, even given what
happened, Bob's recklessness could not possibly have been
Andrew's influence, Andrew now always bedraggled and
sludging through the breezeways of the complex, always
now alone, forlorn, bereft, such that you could stop him
and give to him a "Hey, what's going on," and he would
exchange it for silence. That's Andrew and Andrew's lot,
and this is not an acknowledgment that I had any influence over Andrew or how he might be thornlike to all of
us with his malcontent by pulling us back into the unfortunate past after the catastrophe, or that he may have
been willful in his dolor even before the incident, and neither can I try to explain nor justify the thin smile that
remains fixed to his blushless face as he drifts throughout the complex on the internal two-tiered breezeway that
ringed the pool, declining various offers and condolences
from all of us. We've all taken things hard, but it is not for
Andrew to play the martyr.

I wanted to make things clear to you. I don't want you to believe that Andrew played the main part in what happened, but you should know that Andrew was closest to Bob, like brothers, as they say, almost like twins, and that each one of us has weaknesses of personality and that those weaknesses can, when searched for, be easily found. It could be said that there was an element of us egging each other on during the incident and now perhaps a refusal to handle the present, and that Andrew met the latter with a distribution of shrugs.

Nor is this an apology. I don't feel that it's mine to give. I did my part in what happened in the incident, which was on the surface pure misbehavior by all parts, as you must soon concur, but, in any event, my part was but a part and nothing more. I was a participant. This is not a confession of guilt, although I do feel remorse, because it would be inhuman not to feel something over what happened to Bob, by which I mean the drowning, but the authorities are sure, I want to let you know, that it came to nothing like anyone, even Andrew, holding Bob's head under the water or willing into actuality what took place. The death was ruled misadventure. I played my part and the rope belonged to me, but I didn't purchase the liquor or even suggest the exercise, which in fact was suggested by Bob himself, having spied a documentary on the Navy SEALs in which there was a strenuous test of athletic ability and willpower—and it was quite beyond us and beyond even our intentions when Vincent said, well, if you want to prove you can do it, let's find out, no time like the present.

As I've already indicated, the authorities concluded it

was an accident. We've come to an agreement that it was negligence due in part to our drunken state and that we all share the guilt (such as it is) among us, those of us distracted by the fireworks display while Bob plunged, saying, and I can still hear his voice clearly: "Guys, watch me, I can really do this, I was a champion swimmer at Indiana State." But we can't blame the alcohol any more than we can blame our agreement with Bob that this would be a good bet, and I'm disinclined to say whether in my heart I thought it was the right thing to do because I must admit my thoughts had not touched right or wrong that festive night, much less safe or unsafe.

I was the partygoer poolside with the rope, however, rope I still had in my closet from hauling a mattress on my Honda a few weeks prior, a new one to replace what happened to its predecessor when Alex stayed over and things got out of hand. Which is an incident I will pass over to spare time and mutual embarrassment. I supplied the rope that bound Bob's hands and feet, or rather wrists and ankles, but I did not prepare the rope nor do the actual tying, which was a task left partly to Vincent (the ankles) but primarily to Adam (the wrists and the cutting of the rope in proper lengths), and it was our intention that we would take turns, each of us trying to prove himself in the manner of a Navy SEAL, after a certain jesting fashion. I want to assure you that it was all meant in good fun and was not planned in any part beforehand and even, as I mentioned above, was Bob's suggestion, though we had all viewed the documentary *Go Hard: The Life of a NAVY SEAL* on The Learning Channel a few weeks earlier at Bob's place in the complex, having chipped in to order a large deluxe pizza with extra cheese.

It may help you to understand if I explain the exercise. SEALs in training were, in a certain segment of the documentary, bound hand and foot (hands behind the back) and directed to dive into a deep swimming pool and retrieve swimming goggles that had been placed there by the instructors. The intent of this challenge was, I believe, for the SEALs to demonstrate mental toughness and physical strength and dexterity, though a test of lungpower might also have been at play. I don't remember the program clearly, though I do remember Bob pointing to the screen and saying, "That looks easy, I could do that," and the rest of us telling him no, that it was more difficult than it looked, that if the prospective SEALs were having difficulty with it, then it would be far beyond the literal and metaphorical reach of an ordinary civilian, even if he used to be a champion swimmer at Indiana State. But back to the program: the SEALs dove down headfirst, bound, and retrieved the goggles either with their toes or with their teeth. I must confess we were inebriated when we watched the program, so my memory is not clear. What I can relay to you is that when Bob brought the subject up again poolside on July 3 during our party, it was Bob's idea that he should use his teeth, and as we didn't have an extra pair of swimming goggles for Bob to dive for, we would use a piece of the rope tied to a small donut-shaped weight, and I am not sure how the weight materialized, but I believe it belonged to Andrew. No one claimed it after the incident.

And I don't feel as if I should belabor you with every detail but instead simply give you the report, so that you should know and hence come to your own conclusion. All six of us were inebriated; it was approximately 9:30 p.m. when Bob made his suggestion and I fetched the rope and scissors and Andrew (?) fetched the weight and Adam and Vincent tied the rope to the weight and let it sink at the pool's deep end and then led Bob up to the diving board, at the base of which his wrists and ankles were bound to each other, wrist to wrist, ankle to ankle. He then, with a slow shuffling motion given his restricted stride, moved to the edge of the diving board, and although it was darkening at that point and our complex is not very well lit, I recall him turning back to us and smiling and saying, "Hey, guys, here I go." And of course, mentioning again his swimming prowess. After that he plunged headfirst, bouncing himself off the board and into the deep in a wide arc. Just then, however, a fireworks display celebrating the holiday commenced very near to our complex, and we all turned away from Bob to watch.

After a few moments, and I can't say with any certainty how long it was, Andrew called back to Bob to give it up and come watch the fireworks, which incidentally were magnificent and left us in awe of red and blue melting jellyfish starbursts superimposed upon each other in the sky for a few jubilant moments. There was no call of defeat or triumph from Bob, however, and Andrew turned back to watch, assuming Bob would rise with up without the weight. After a few more moments, several of us turned back again to spot Bob, who was still in the pool.

Andrew and Adam and I moved from where we were on the deck chairs to get a closer look, and what we found was Bob, in a tilted column, floating head-side-up close to the bottom of the pool, motionless. Adam and I dove in to lift him out of the water, each of us at an elbow, and we bent his still-bound body over the pool's edge. After a few rudimentary shakes, we were certain that Bob wasn't simply playing a cruel joke, so Alex began CPR and Vincent dialed 911.

Of course things did not turn out well for us that night, not least of which for Bob, but when the EMT summoned the police and they questioned us, we told them about the program and the boast, and they (and we) all agreed that it was odd that he didn't even at least rise to the pool's surface, but that in any case it was an accident. Death by misadventure, rather. All of us in the complex who knew each other well enough to hail the others as friends felt deeply distressed and aggrieved about the entire situation, and all of us rehearsed scenarios in which we could have persuaded him not to go through with the boast, or, if you would have it differently, the dare. I should mention that the funeral was solemn and ostentatious, a flood of lilies surrounding the mahogany casket in the dim velvet room, and that all of us participants and friends attended and were acquitted of blame by Bob's family, with Bob's father even saying, "We always knew Bob was reckless, and that when he went, it would be this kind of thing," though of course everyone had been hoping for a long life and a death by natural causes with only a few reckless acts to share as stories told to Bob's friends and family and future life partner and children, were he to elect to have them. This is to say that in a certain sense Bob's death was to be expected, but that nevertheless it shook us all.

Q. Why doesn't Martin feel the need to apologize? Q. Why does Martin describe Andrew at such length? Q. What could have contributed to the others' willingness to help Bob perform his stunt? Q. Even given the fireworks and the drunkenness, why did the group suddenly become so unobservant? Q. What is Martin trying to achieve in reporting everyone's agreement about Bob's recklessness?

SEPTEMBER

One report following hard upon another is a decided strain, but I must inform you of what happened to Andrew, poor Andrew, wounded the most of all of us by Bob's death, although he was not the main player in the sorrow of that holiday night. Approximately six weeks after Bob was buried, Andrew stopped attending our frequent social functions in the complex, both casual and formal. At first we thought he was nursing his grief privately, and we gave him due space. In time, though, we became concerned given that Andrew's car was never seen to move from the complex's lot—yet when Alex knocked, nearly pounded, on Andrew's door, there was no answer. After a day or two of knowing the facts of the car and the lack of answer, we decided to call the landlord and report our collective concern about the welfare of our friend and that he wasn't answering his door. The building manager let us in to Andrew's apartment, and it was in the bathroom we found him having hanged himself with the rope from our terrible night from the heavy steel curtain support beam of the shower. The building manager remarked that he must have suffered to go slowly like that and told us that he would take care of things and that we should wait outside the apartment.

The police arrived again, and again we explained the Bob incident and the origin of the rope and ventured that Andrew may have hanged himself bereft for lack of Bob and remorseful over the whole enterprise and the small part he played in it. Of course, we were all shaken badly. There was no explanatory note. And I will pass over the description of Andrew, poor, slight Andrew, dangling from the shower curtain support beam, knees grazing the tub-edge, given the support beam's low height and Andrew's lanky frame, but I should impress upon you that it was a sight that won't soon leave my mind or the minds of our friends. Indeed, some of us began musing aloud about moving out of the building, a building with too many bad memories, two sorry deaths. Adam, for one, suggested that he was thinking seriously about relocating. I decided to stay, though, because of the on-the-main convenience of the location and the knowledge that surely things would end with Andrew after the funeral, at which we explained the Bob incident to Andrew's tearful mother and stoic younger brother. At the complex we began to meet less frequently for social occasions, and so I was compelled to develop new relationships, both with others in the complex and with men I met online.

For a while, then, there was some resettlement, but

things continued somewhat as they had during Andrew's curious absence, and inasmuch as all of us privately harbored thoughts of having reached out to Andrew or in some other way done something to save him from his terrible fate, there was simply nothing any of us could do but move on and, as with Bob's incident, become more watchful over ourselves, our friends, and our collective behavior. I do, however, recall a passage of conversation with Bob before his decease, during which he confessed that he had misgivings about Andrew's mental health, and that conversation still gives me qualms, primarily because it had the import of the hushed passage of key information, yet neither of us acted upon what we knew, Bob obviously being unable to do so after his death. Briefly, then, things returned to a semblance of normalcy, while we individually were put upon to consider our own lives and directions and try to understand what drove both Bob and Andrew to their distinct but still unfathomable decisions.

Q. Why does Martin pass over the "details" of the suicide itself? Q. What might be some reasons this report is much shorter and in a less formal diction than the first report? Q. Does it make sense for Martin to stay in the building if it holds so many bad memories? Q. Why doesn't Martin adequately account for his feelings about the suicide? Q. Why is the report of Andrew's funeral passed over?

MARCH

This, now, after a considerable length of silence, is less of a confession than a simple addition to the file on the course of our fates here on San Vincente, a report to give you the uncensored story of my own actions within the context of the deaths and what transpired in the weeks and months following Andrew's funeral. The quietly aired intimations of moving rendered themselves into facts, and over the next months, all of our usual gang save myself (the others from whom you may have heard individual reports) left the complex to resettle at nearby complexes or duplexes in the city. This unfolded gradually, and there were promises made that we would all stay in touch, but those promises faded with the ensuing weeks as what once was a circle of friends brought together by proximity loosened until it dissolved entirely. This is not to say that I don't still hold occasional phone conversations with Vincent, Adam, or Alex, but that things now are merely incidental to our collective past fellowship. There is a quality of strain in our asking after each other's activities and outcomes. And of course our salutations are becoming less and less frequent as the days whisk by us and we drift into our diverse futures. Hence this is not a confession of guilt or insinuation of error, but rather a report meant to deliver you the entire, as they say, unvarnished truth of what is happening, now that my proximal friends have slid quietly away and I am still seeking to understand the incidents—Andrew's less than Bob's because of the relative lack of mystery on Andrew's part, other than direct motive, but it is not for us to know, entirely, you must concur, what blossoms in the minds of others, as hard as we might try. And try we must.

After my contact with my old friends became tenuous,

I began to forge new friendships via the Internet. As you are of course aware, I am relatively young and modestly comely and I strive to maintain an athletic build, and I sought the company of a number of men in the months following the end of our formal social circle. At first these were simply matters on the level of so-called first dates, nothing of them to relay other than that they proceeded with all the awkwardness and hesitation, explicit or implicit, as any first date carries. And it should be noted that there were many first dates and no second or third dates. This was by intent. A relationship was not what I was seeking, even given the pleasure and promise I found in a few of the men with whom I had dinner or accompanied on varieties of taking-the-pressure-off day outings.

Gradually, the encounters became more exploratory. At first I began to invite men back to my apartment in the complex for drinks after dates, and I would casually tell them an "acquaintance" who had lived here had drowned, bound hand and foot, and I would supply this as a topic for conversation, probing the innocent men variously according to their personalities and inclinations as to how it must have felt for dear Bob and what must have gone wrong so badly to induce Andrew to suicide. These conversations were somewhat difficult, not least because it was an awkward subject to introduce. Most of the men merely remarked at what an awful thing it must have been to have witnessed the events at close hand and offered the polite empathy of strangers before bidding me farewell.

Finally, then, in what for me was an admittedly bold

move, I dispensed with the formality of the dates and bought some rope, a swimsuit resembling Bob's blue Speedo, and the brand of swimming goggles he wore. I roamed a different set of websites catering to different male needs and asked other varieties of men over to my apartment, informing them exactly where my interests lay. I didn't get a great many responses, but the ones I received were filled with eagerness, and so commenced my investigation of the incident in earnest, queries made in order to know and report what goes on in the minds of other men. After what happened to unfortunate Bob, however, I was reluctant to go near the swimming pool other than to pass by it, glancing elsewhere, on my way to my one-bedroom abode, so when the men arrived at the gate and I ushered them into my apartment and invited them to disrobe and then don the swimsuit and goggles, I used the rope I had bought to bind them, wrists and ankles, and sat them in a chair with their ankles tied to a crossbar beneath the chair and their wrists tied together behind the chair back and down to the same crossbar. Then, I must report for the sake of being comprehensive, I told them I was planning to hold my hands over their nose and mouth for a few seconds on and off, ten or twelve seconds at most, nothing dangerous, and ask them to inform me how they would feel if they were bound like this and about to drown. Some of the men balked though I proceeded anyway, and some were more imaginative than others in giving me the diverse and often surprising answers I sought, but all of them, to the last (and this was nearly a dozen men), told me, in one form or another, pull down my swimming trunks and take hold of me and I'll tell you anything you want to know.

Q. Why does Martin feel obligated to report such personal information? Q. Why do you suppose Martin mentions his early dating? Q. Why might Martin have gone to such elaborate lengths to reenact a scene and oblige the men sexually? Q. Is any part of what happened in all three reports possibly eroticized for Martin? Q. What do you suppose are some of the things the men told him after he allowed them to breathe again?

LIARS

CARL N.
Told me that two wrongs don't make a right.

MY NEIGHBOR BOB (WHO'S AN EX-MARINE)
Explained to me it was a matter of the power of positive thinking, and that the worst thing I could do was shoot myself in the foot before I even got off the boat. (I liked talking to Bob.)

JASON K.
Told me that sex was a beautiful and magical thing, that it was the pinnacle of life's experience of pleasure, and that

there was more to it than him simply sticking his dick up my ass, that even on the basic, prosaic level of lovemaking there was mouth-to-genital contact and different kinds of genital-to-genital contact, not to mention all the different stuff you can do with your hands.

THE COUNTY OFFICE
Informed me via letter I wasn't quite poor enough to qualify as "Poor."

ME
Told myself that I could work with the money I had, and that lots of people were happy despite their poverty.

MY YOUNGER SISTER
Told me my hair would recover if I did what I did to it.

JASON K.
Also told me that sex was mostly in a person's mind, and to give in to the moment, and that there was more to it than just the awkward sweating and clutching of it, and that he wouldn't even go near my ass if I wasn't comfortable with it, even though I still ended up with my face pressed into the corduroy couch cushions and with my bare ass sticking up (it felt like) and with Jason trying to wrangle his dick into my ass, which wasn't cooperating. He said there was no reason to worry.

SEVERAL BILLING DEPARTMENTS
Suggested the blame was entirely mine.

THE LEAD SINGER OF MY FAVORITE BAND
Sang that *regret saves lives.* I want to write him a letter to ask him if he can provide specifics on this—case histories and so forth—but I'm not the letter-writing kind.

GEORGE
Told me that being in danger makes life more interesting.

THE STAFF OF THE HEALING CENTER
Convinced me to move out there because they said it would make my future more comfortable.

MY BROTHER AND SISTER
Convinced me to move home because at least then, they said, I would feel like I was at home.

THE NURSE
Told me it would hurt less if I looked away.

THIS GUY STEVE I KNOW WHO'S A DRAG QUEEN BUT ACTUALLY STRAIGHT
Told me that the solution was finding a healthy outlet where I could stop focusing on my problems and jump into a different world (and asked me if I could lip-sync and walk in heels).

THE COLLECTION AGENCY
Sent me letters telling me my problems could be solved now with just one reduced lump sum.

MY CHILDHOOD FRIENDS
Told me that I was a baby for crying so much, that everyone died sooner or later, that if I were more like them I would get over it, though they didn't say how long it would take.

THE HOME HOSPICE STAFF
Assured me that yes, you could die with dignity.

MELANIE H. AND STEVEN R.
Had me almost convinced that some things (diamonds, but also truth and beauty) are forever when we stayed up all night smoking a bowl and drinking two-buck chuck after the high school graduation party petered out.

JACK KEROUAC
Wrote somewhere, I think, that the key was to live your dreams and let happiness happen. That might not have been Kerouac, though. Might have been Oprah.

ME
Told myself that I had done everything within my power.

PEOPLE WHO WRITE FOR THE PAPERS AND MAGAZINES I GLANCE AT IN WAITING ROOMS
Want to inform me that being *indigent* isn't necessarily a life sentence. (These people, who phrase things in terms of prison, seem afraid to use the word "poor.")

SEVERAL LEADING ECONOMIC THEORISTS
Maintain that while class is certainly an important factor in the general warp and curvature of a person's life, it doesn't represent as much of a factor as individual *drive* and *determination* (they talk about these things as if they were different, or complementary), as well as good, old-fashioned American luck.

THE GUY AT THE CLINIC WITH THE BLUE HAIR
Told me that the nature of luck is that everybody has both at some point, good and bad.

STEVE THE DRAG QUEEN
Told me I was lucky because I had the lips of a woman, specifically the sexy pout of Greta Garbo, and that it would open doors for me even if I didn't know exactly how to work it.

THIS GUY WHOSE NAME I THINK WAS RICHARD
Told me in the small motel room that the greater the risk, the more satisfying the reward. Think of acrobats, he said.

JOHN S. AND TYLER P. AND A FEW OTHER PEOPLE
Told me that they loved me, and implied that it was important.

DOUGLAS
Said that more guys would fuck me the way I wanted it and not just perfunctorily if only I seemed less somber.

EVERYBODY
Says it helps to "Look on the bright side."

THE PRESIDENT OF THE UNITED STATES OF AMERICA
Said that yes I can.

LORNA H.
Told me that things wouldn't change between us, even if I really were sick.

MY UNCLE RON
Gave me a newspaper clipping about the relationship between medicine and spirituality and told me to think about it.

MY PRIEST (WHO I HADN'T SEEN
SINCE I WAS TWELVE)
Told me that it was in God's hands, and that God loves everyone, and that even though I hadn't technically done anything much to repent for, as far as he knew, that it wouldn't hurt to go to confession anyway, just in case there was anything I needed to get off my chest, because although God loves everyone, He, just like a lot of mortals, has a limit.

MY FRIENDS AND RELATIVES
Suggested that there was a lesson to be learned in all of this somewhere.

ME

Told myself that there was a lesson to be learned in all of this somewhere.

MY MOTHER

Told me it would be easier if I kept some things to myself.

MY NEW DOCTOR (WHO SMELLED
FAINTLY OF CINNAMON)

Told me that everything was going to be OK, ultimately, and that it was a matter of taking care of myself. That taking care of myself (though he didn't specify what that entailed, exactly, as he tugged at his lab coat and tried to look comprehensively educated) was not just a necessity, but a responsibility. He told me that I was lucky, relatively, and that it was a matter of taking responsibility for myself, which implied that that would make a difference.

THE BANK

Initially told me that I hadn't overdrawn my account.

HAMISH L.

Told me that breathing deeply would help, that everything was going to be OK, and that he'd only touch me where I wanted him to, that we had all the time in the world, and that there was no need to worry, and that the best way to look at it was: how could things possibly get any worse?

LABOR

They both agreed he'd stay tied to the chair for the full eight hours because that was a day's work and what they were doing wasn't play anymore, at least not for both of them, but after he got tied to the chair like they agreed and he got gagged, the other man pulled up a chair facing him and said well, now, let's negotiate.

NIGHTFALL

While the sun sinks behind a squat black strip mall across the street, Doug and his boyfriend are playing a game with their complimentary packets of syrup at the local IHOP. Doug's boyfriend Evan had grown up near the IHOP and the game is his, the object being to come up with the most toxic mix of fruit-based syrups possible. The game had been an annual opening night ritual after high school plays when Evan was in Drama Club. When Evan explained the game to Doug, he couldn't recall who came up with it, though he thought it might have been Cindy, the future civil engineer who wasn't out of the closet yet. The winner is the person who can stomach

a concoction that his adversaries can't, and Doug's boyfriend is an old pro, and it's his old game, so Doug's letting
him win, making a face he knew would convince Evan
and protesting that the peach/chocolate/maple combina-
tion is out of his league.

The waitress is eyeing them as she serves the other cus-
tomers (Doug and his boyfriend have been there a long
time—Evan likes to mull over his strategy), but Doug
doesn't care; his boyfriend seems happy, and all Doug
wants is to see him content, even if it means spending an
evening at his childhood IHOP in a neighborhood that's
not quite as suburban as it used to be. And it seems lucky
to Doug that he's sitting facing the window while his boyfriend sits facing him, because he knows Evan wouldn't
be pleased by what Doug can see past him through the
veils of dusk light, which is: leaves blowing, a wet-looking
dog running from left to right and then back to the left
again, and a man in a baggy suit, near the dirty glass of
the other side of the IHOP window but not quite touching it. Even from a distance the stranger seems tense, to
Doug at least, or else poised, ready for some sudden burst.
Doug had grown used to seeing a similar tension in his
boyfriend after the attack, and he's glad that Evan is content to pass the time with Doug there, drinking black cof-
fee, picking at his pancakes, and playing the game, not
needing to think about anything in particular, past or
future. He's especially glad that, because of everything
Evan had been through, he didn't have the sense to notice
Doug looking over his shoulder at the stranger beyond the
glass, Doug keeping an eye on him as he sticks his finger

in the maple/strawberry and makes another little show of being disgusted. Evan's request to come here—he'd been asking about it since waking up in the hospital—had been odd, since he hadn't been here in years, and the neighborhood had obviously changed almost beyond recognition, and he didn't know anyone here anymore. Though he didn't really even seem to notice the neighborhood at all. Even on the drive over, his eyes had been closed because, he'd said, the sunset was painful, and he'd resumed humming along to an innocuous oldie on the car radio that Doug recognized but couldn't place, Evan having spent a childhood listening to his parents' LPs now just barely old enough to qualify as oldie. Not that this was a bad neighborhood, but after Evan had been attacked, Doug had a hard time believing in the goodness of any neighborhood, even if it wasn't here on the far north side but downtown where a man, evidently having not taken his medication (or so the police said), had attacked Doug's boyfriend with a knife as he left work.

Doug looks past Evan, one of whose scars is visible— a red thread reaching up beyond the lip of the thin blue turtleneck sweater Doug had bought him last Christmas and that he wore a lot now, he said, because he liked it, because it reminded him of the thick turtleneck sweaters he wore as a kid even after his family moved south from Escanaba in Upper Michigan to Milwaukee in time for Evan to go to a decent high school, but also out of embarrassment over the scar—and Doug notes that the stranger is still out there, looking in. By now the light has shifted enough for the man outside to be little more than a silhouette. He is still there, though, and as his boyfriend picks at a finger-thick, slightly skillet-burnt pancake, Doug considers the question of whether the stranger would leave or not, and what to do if he stuck around, and how to get Evan back into the car and head homeward in the rapidly arriving dark without him having to realize any perceived threats, even if they were all in his or Doug's heads. The attack in the street had been random, a local news-hour lead story for a day or so, an incident unlikely to be replicated, and the man who'd attacked Evan was still in custody and undergoing evaluation, but as Doug watches his scar-covered boyfriend grin sort of sheepishly and lean over to stick his tongue into a small blob of strawberry/peach/maple, he wonders what it means to make those kinds of plans now, after something so random had happened, what it means to be there now, and how to get home, and how to prevent (or at least minimize) the role of chance in their future life, from tonight onward.

After a while, happy to spend the time there with Evan, who's winning, Doug begins to think that the man outside, who didn't seem as if he were planning to go anywhere anytime soon, seems as if he were looking at Doug and not the other way around. And then, as his boyfriend smiles sedately through his string of victories and straightens up a bit from his hunch, it starts to seem to Doug as if it isn't the man outside that seemed unusually tense but the whole sunset itself, which is wetly red and which had reduced Evan to shades of gray, a handsome and rounded outline, before the IHOP lights took over and darkened the exterior. It looks to Doug like tapes he had

seen on nature shows of fast-forward time-lapse night-
falls, a blur of lost time, and he's happy that Evan isn't
aware that time is passing outside so wildly, that things
out there in the world are still happening, good or bad,
and happening fast, and Doug's pleasure in Evan's ignorance makes him lean toward him across the booth table,
put his hand on Evan's arm (which seemed cold under the
sweater) and, even though he is supposed to be gleefully
disgusted, force a calm smile and tell Evan again how
happy he is that things are fine now and they are there together, nothing to worry about at all.

PUSH PUSH PUSH

FACT: The thing I was thinking about, in the five seconds before the driver's side front corner of my 2002 Camry gave a good hard clunk to the passenger's side corner of the car diagonally to the left and in front of me, was: Nietzsche. I think. I don't know much about Nietzsche, other than that he's dead and German and I might have covered him in some class in college, but what I was thinking instead of counting to ten like I knew I was supposed to was that thing, the line, something about how whatever doesn't kill you makes you stronger, if I have it right, and it seemed odd, in Tuesday rush-hour traffic, to know just that one quote and almost nothing else. Later in the hospital I was thinking about the Levinas thing I do remember from college, about the Thou, about being for the other before being for yourself, if I still have that straight, and I guess that maybe would've been more helpful anger-management-wise, but Levinas isn't exactly as entrenched as a catchphrase in our culture. So I was cruising along a little angry or maybe more than a little angry and thinking Nietzsche.

Then I sped up a bit and jerked the wheel to the left to see if what I thought was going to happen would happen.

FACT: I watch too much TV. Is what my girlfriend tells me. I call her my *live-in girlfriend* when I'm joking around, trying to piss her off because of how frequently she spends nights at my apartment, which is closer to where she goes to school than hers is. Live-in, I say, go fetch me a beer. She gets mock-pissed off because I'm such a dumb sexist, but then we both laugh because I don't mean it, really. I don't even drink beer, except on social occasions, and sitting around the house watching too much of whatever it is I'm watching is not a social occasion, even when my live-in is there in the evenings during prime TV viewing hours, which she usually isn't because she has school stuff almost all the time now, night and day, and I just have the 9-to-5 fluorescent cubicle grind.

My girlfriend's studying to be a doctor, which, while I agree with her that it's noble and lucrative and everything, considering the market for it—considering the reliability of illness—makes me a little nervous. Secretly, the idea of her rubbing hands over me that a few hours earlier were injecting or slicing up sick people brimming over with god-only-knows-what creeps me out a little. I suggested she become a teacher because she's good with kids, and it probably would involve less risk of contamination (though I guess you never know) and, tacitly, creepiness, but she said as much as she likes kids, eight or more hours of them a day is too much, and she doesn't see how people can do it. Plus, the kind of doctor she's becoming—neurosurgeon—is not very hands-on, or rather it is very hands-on but not very patient-heavy, she reminds me.

I like her. A lot. I like how she's cheerful but not in that crazy zealous kind of way, I like her warm, calm, levelheaded body next to mine, I like how she straddles me and gives me what she calls her "hair shower," shaking her head to brush my unshaven face with her long red hair that smells like exotic fruit. I think we're probably going to get married, though of course after the incident everything's open to question, but for my part, once my legs heal and the legal things are settled and everything, I'd be willing. She already knows I'm like this anyway, more or less. Or at least capable of it. At least I think she knows. And if she knows, she must be OK with it, I think.

FACT: The thing about the TV I watch too much of is that it's always these trashy, low-grade Real Crime things I'm a little embarrassed to get so hooked on—*Amazing Police Videos* and "dramatizations" of bank robberies and historically daring prison escapes and such, and the side benefit to it is how much information you can get from watching innocuous cable shows. I mean, I know more about car chases than about Nietzsche, which says something but I'm not sure what. And I could probably rob a bank if I wanted to and I had the proper plan. And a reason to do it. A lot more people get away with a lot more things than you would think, at least I think so, probably statistically speaking, not on camera obviously, but in real life. I've gotten away with plenty, at least until recently.

FACT: I don't know what the other driver was thinking. A short, bald man with an angrily creased head who'd cut me off on not one but two separate occasions, the second accompanied by an extended middle finger silhouetted by the setting sun. The thing that really drove me nuts was that he didn't even look back to see who he was flipping off. I mean I could have been anyone: a nun, or the president, or some kind of psychopath, you name it. Plus he had a vanity license plate that read TOOTS, and that kind of thing is just totally uncalled for.

Not that I didn't deserve the finger, considering the way I drive, but the fact that he didn't even *look* is what was the main problem. Because when you cut someone off in traffic, twice, there's some sort of relationship suggested there, some sort of ad-hoc or tacit acknowledgment that there's some sort of thread there between you and the other guy, I and Thou, his fat head with a red haze around it because of the sunset, the backlit glint of all the other cars making you squint and twitch a little as you narrow your vision and make certain hasty decisions that end up complicating your life in exactly the wrong way.

FACT: One of the things I learned as a result of watching too much *Real Police Action* and *Cops* is how officers are trained to stop a car containing a car thief or crazy person or other individual who needs to be stopped in order to preserve the safety of the presumably innocent folks in the vicinity. It's called the PITT Maneuver, and I think those letters are an acronym, though I don't know what for. What the officers do is pull up diagonally behind the car in question, overlapping a little, and then basically change lanes very quickly, sending the car containing the must-be-stopped person or people into a tailspin that provides the officers with valuable seconds of disorientation and slowdown to move on in and surround the alleged.

The tricky part in this maneuver, I found out, is maintaining control of your own car, which is just as likely to spin or veer if you're not trained and thinking clearly, the rear of your car swinging counterclockwise while the bald asshole spins clockwise up ahead of you and people change lanes and honk horns, and the otherwise surprisingly light rush-hour traffic grinds to a twilight halt. And then bang, you're sideways on a highway and here comes a Chevy Avalanche with soft brakes.

I wasn't thinking about that leading up to the actual incident, though, obviously. I was thinking about Nietzsche, briefly, and about how my favorite part of those cop shows are when the officers swarm the innocent-until-proven-guilty, their firearms drawn, and pull him or her or them out of the spun-around car and swarm and kneel on and cuff them and transport them off with a sense of the same kind of tension and annoyance that I feel at my job, as if everybody knew how it was going to end anyway, why bother with a chase?

FACT: I tried to get my live-in to play cops and robbers with me once and handcuff me to the bed with these real, authentic police cuffs I bought off Handcuffwarehouse .com, but the whole thing turned out to be kind of awkward and my wrists started to hurt, so she ended up ditching the police stuff I'd bought and sitting next to me on the bed with my hands still cuffed, jacking me off while I shut my eyes and replayed scenes of dramatizations in my head, me as both perpetrator and enforcer. More perpetrator than enforcer, though, probably, given it was sort of obvious and unspoken from the start that I was the one who'd get cuffed.

After that we silently threw all that stuff out in a black Hefty even though the authentic cuffs had set me back a solid twenty (plus shipping and handling) and the police stuff had cost even more. This just isn't us, she'd said after I came and she uncuffed me and I wiped off, and I'd nodded in what I hoped looked like agreement.

FACT: I don't know why I was thinking about Nietzsche. I'm not the philosophical type, really. I'm very action-oriented, as was noted in my annual job performance review, though my boss said sometimes too action-oriented, and I wanted to ask what she meant but didn't.

COMMENTARY: Which is to say, I'm not the sort who sits around scratching his ass and thinking about the big pic-

ture. I'm a moment-to-moment kind of guy. But this thing
with the guy, the driver, TOOTS, was simply the last little moment in a series of moments that had been accumu-
lating for quite some while. I mean, it's not like nobody's
ever given me the finger before or cut me off in traffic, but
there was something about how badly I wanted to let this
asshole know how I didn't need to be in a hurry, but how
I did like to pass really slow, grandma-driven cars like he
did, but not quite at the same rate, and how the bottle-
neck I briefly caused had less to do with willful behavior on my part than something wrong with the gearshift
of the car (which I need to get checked out when I get the
chance, if the car is fixable) and how generally it was the
kind of day where if anyone notices you at all, it's because
you've fucked something up.

Not that I fucked anything up that day, up until the incident. Maybe that's why I did it, other than just out of
sheer curiosity. And not counting to ten first. And on record it was an accident, of course. I simply changed lanes
while misjudging the space available. And I hope the people who need to believe that do believe that, including
TOOTS, though he is nonetheless filing suit and probably
has no idea who Nietzsche even is, though I think there
was a football player with a similar name and that's probably more the asshole's kind of thing, if he has a thing and
doesn't just sit around all day with his thumb up his ass,
lonely and angry and loud.

But in any case, the flash through my mind was that
even if this would not make me stronger, it would at least
leave a mark, so to speak, add an exclamation point to the

sentence in my tight head. I didn't have any personal malicious intent per se.

FACT: At least not much malicious intent. Not a *statistically significant quantity*, if you know what I mean. Just the normal amount.

FACT: Earlier that day, my live-in called me at the office to tell me the good news: that she had been accepted into the residency program she wanted to get into at Kansas in Lawrence. I'd tried on numerous occasions to tell her that this was *Kansas*, and that Kansas didn't even have indoor plumbing much less *residency programs* in neurosurgery. But she visited there and liked it and said it was calm and friendly, that it was tidy and spacious and there were actual buildings several stories tall and Starbucks and Jamba Juice and it wasn't all rusty tractors, trailer parks, and husky men in overalls chewing tobacco and kind of staring at you like, what is someone like you doing here, and that she wanted to know what it was like to live there (she said she *enjoyed the change of pace*), so that meant that the possibility of having to move to Kansas had hardened into some kind of kernel of something that, on the phone, was making me have a hard time swallowing, and I'd already had to deal with Kendrick taking two goddamn hours to photocopy the Gladson case report for eleven waiting people.

Of course I was happy for her, but I hated how she kept making me have to make decisions about my future. Our future. I knew if I suggested coasting on what she had and doing her residency locally, because there was my own employment to consider and we're talking a big commute from Lawrence to any city of any size, she would take it the wrong way, as selfishness versus practicality, and might not talk to me for a few days, or worse, so I tried to make my voice sound like I was smiling and told her that if Dorothy wanted to get back there so much it couldn't be all bad, but on the other hand, if I had to get up in the middle of the night and use an outdoor john and subscribe to Creationism, then that was the end of it.

She knew I was kidding, of course. She was laughing when she hung up the phone.

FACT: The way things spun when our wheels touched was such that what you could see past the rim of the highway side-barrier—an endless landscape of green and brown fields, brown and gray trees, and gray buildings, all slurred orange-red by the setting sun—whirled in a way that formed a dull gray-blue stripe of highway wall under the unevenly light orange-gray stripe of the sky and the alternately dark and shiny mottled stripe of car spin and sudden halt going on around me. The stripe of the landscape looked like a thing you could reach out and grab. I wondered if TOOTS was thinking the same thing, or whether he had his eyes closed, as people sometimes do when they hear loud noises, because it *was* loud, or are confronted with unexpected incidents. Accidents.

FACT: Not that he could've considered it all that unexpected if he were really, *really* paying attention, but the deal is that he wasn't paying attention at all, just push push push.

COMMENTARY: I figure a corollary to the whole Nietzsche thing that whoever ends up in the most pain wins, literally or metaphorically, and I figure that, by that token, when you consider all the different kinds of pain in the world, the winner in this particular situation was me, and then that it was probably meant to be my turn to win, since when the cars first hit and spun the deep thud of the metal sounded, for an instant, not like an accident, but like two lost things that were always meant to fit together finally making contact. Hand in glove.

THIS IS NOT A ROMANCE

The last time I saw Billy was under an enormous trellis arch in my parents' summer house garden, twelve feet high and ten feet wide, and he was seated on one of the two curved stone benches beneath it and was playing Solitaire with a deck of tarot cards he had used to foretell my fate a month back. He stood when he saw me arrive, and he held my sides with his warm, thick-fingered hands and smiled, and I said, "What happens now?"

I spent most of my summer at the house not really wondering *what happens now.*

He had told me his name was Billy, but once when he was sleeping, I slipped his driver's license out of his wallet, and the name on it was Thomas Parker.

I met Billy at a bar I went to every once in a while early that summer; I was too young to be allowed in, but the bar owners and bartenders knew who my parents were so they let me stay, and I was a slow, careful drinker and not obnoxious, so they never bothered me.

The way he smiled at me, almost a smirk.

One night Billy was at the bar and walked up to me sitting in a booth alone and said, you look like you're a very interesting person, and I told him I had never given it much thought, and he sat down across from me and smiled and said, the thing about interesting people is that they are very attractive, and then he asked me what kind of drink he could buy me and suggested that since this was Long Island it should be a Long Island Iced Tea.

I had already lost my virginity at Princeton to a skinny math major named Gilbert Wainwright the year before. It was at a party, not a frat party, because that was not our scene, but something more low-key, and we simply looked at each other, and we left the living room and found a bedroom, and we didn't talk much and I sucked his cock and he sucked mine, and we spat each other out on Jacob Epstein's nubby-carpeted floor.

Before Billy, my sexual experiences tended to be furtive and lackluster.

Billy officially stayed in the forest-themed guest room on the first floor, but we spent most nights in my bed, full-sized, large enough to accommodate us both but only barely.

I spent summers alone at the house starting when I was fifteen because my parents left for Europe every summer and didn't want to bring me along and didn't want me to get into any trouble. Mostly I spent the summers reading books and, once I got older, reading books and drinking a beer or two at the bar a few miles away.

My room was filled with scattered books I hadn't finished yet or had given up on altogether.

All Billy brought with him was one large black duffel bag. No car of his own.

We never ran out of condoms, even though I never remember him buying any and I hadn't brought any of my own with me. Billy requested we use them even for oral, but he wouldn't explain specifically why but noted it was not disease-related. I didn't ask because as long as we fucked and it felt good, it didn't matter.

In the garden the last time I saw him, he said that he was right, and I asked him what he was talking about, and he said, you really are a very interesting person. I said I still wasn't sure.

Sometimes I'd lie awake in bed with Billy while he slept, and I would look at him and wonder whether this kind of thing was anything approaching ordinary, and I decided it probably wasn't, and then I decided I probably didn't really mind.

I never asked Billy about his name. I never asked about a lot of things.

I told Billy we could bareback. I trusted him and could get tested for whatever when I was back at Princeton, but he said no. I wanted to get as close to him as two people could get.

I never thought of myself as a very interesting person.

The last time I saw Billy and he held me and kissed me standing over his tarot cards and told me to continue to be interesting, I asked him why he was leaving, and he just laughed, and I asked him where he was going, and he said back to New York, probably.

Most of the books that came with the house's library were decorative only. Interior-decorated instead of bought.

At the tarot reading the card representing me was the Magician, which Billy said was good. He interpreted the cross and row of cards he laid out to mean that good fortune was awaiting me, but that it would be a shock and might not reveal itself for years.

I wondered, even before I saw his license, why he was just called Billy and not something more formal.

He never told me his age, but I guessed he was about ten years older than me, probably. Maybe fifteen.

Sometimes we'd use my parents' bed. And leave it rumpled and stained. I knew when they got back they wouldn't even notice, or that by then I'd chicken out and change the sheets.

I still read books during Billy's stay. I got about halfway through *The Brothers Karamazov,* but Billy kept distracting me with meals he'd cook and conversations we'd have and the times when we would fuck, sometimes more than once a day, and take a long time doing it.

What he said when he came was *yes yes yes.* When I came, I closed my eyes and grunted a bit but didn't say anything.

In the garden Billy asked me whether I would consider what we did as a romance. I said I wasn't sure.

My parents were unhappy when I majored in English, though they thought it might be fun for me to work in publishing, but they asked me to double-major in something "serious" as well, and I said I would consider it.

I never really considered it.

My parents were both in the music industry on the behind-the-scenes side, and my mother had also inherited a lot of money and things like the Hamptons house.

Lying in bed with Billy I thought that there was no way I could go back to Gilbert, the skinny mathematics guy, no matter how eager he was to please.

I took care never to do or say much that my parents would know about that might earn their disapproval, other than majoring in English. They were casual when I came out to them because they tried to be hip around me but told me to be careful.

Billy's wavy black hair, and the way I could run my hands through it.

The next summer I spent at the local bar fruitlessly looking for interesting men. Then the summers turned into publishing internships in New York. At least for a while.

In addition to *The Brothers Karamazov*, which I finished after Billy left, I also read *Vanity Fair* and *Moby-Dick* and *Bleak House*. It was mostly a long-book summer. Mostly a nineteenth-century summer. Verdant. Green. Not quite romantic, but it didn't matter much.

The last time I saw Billy, I told him I wasn't sure what a romance was. He said that what happened between us was not it.

I never got tested for anything when I got back to Princeton. And when I got back to Princeton, I had a lot of adult fun.

The way I was, soft and bookish and pale, and how it didn't matter.

The postcard he sent me the following summer, the last I ever heard of him after he gathered up his cards in the garden and put them in his bag and left on foot was a postcard of the leaning tower of Pisa but postmarked Downer's Grove, Illinois, with the simple text, "Hello, I'm not that interesting anymore. But I hope for your sake you're still too young to figure anything out."

And then it was maybe a year later when I started to get sick.

COWBOYS

1. The Basic. Hogtie, face down, wrists tied behind back, ankles tied, wrists tied to ankles.

Depending on the ropework and the location of the knots, this position can range from relatively easy to escape to very difficult, given that both legs and arms are stretched by being pulled together. This is a favorite "warm up" tie for Chris and Dale because they've used it so frequently, and it was one of their first ties they tried on each other when, as kids living in neighboring homes, they played a game of Cowboys and Indians where one day the cowboy was captured and got tied up, an act which interested both boys and turned into a physical challenge game all its own. Chris and Dale devoted their youth to perfecting both tying and escape strategies, and they played the game roughly from when they were eight or nine through their senior year at Cornell, where they were roommates all four years, first in the dorms and then in an apartment.

They referred to the game as the Cowboy Game because of its origins, but it soon became focused on two issues: how skilled Chris or Dale would be at tying the other, and how agile either was at escaping regardless of the tie. When drinking entered the game at college and they had all night to play, plenty of rope, and they were increasingly skilled at tying, they would sometimes take breaks in between ties to drink and talk about school or girls or other things beyond the game. Mostly, though, they traded ties, and these marathons would sometimes stretch from 8 p.m. one night to 10 a.m. the next morning, leaving both men with considerable rope marks and burns (visible on their wrists, most noticeably) that they would either have to cover or come up with ways to explain, usually just dodging the question by claiming not to have noticed the marks and professing to have slept funny, or else confessing to have gotten laid by a kinky girl and then changing the subject. For the most part Chris and Dale kept the game a secret, not because they were ashamed, but because they feared that others might not understand it, even though, for them, the appeal of the challenge was obvious.

When both Chris and Dale married and began families in their late twenties, in the Whitefish Bay suburb of Milwaukee where they grew up, they returned to the game in rented motel rooms, eager to test each other's strength again, while needing to keep things secret to avoid their wives' harboring any kind of suspicion ranging from drug use to strip clubs to adultery. When a guilty-feeling Chris finally told his new wife, Sarah, one day, following some probing from her, her reaction was puzzlement followed by relief. I know you're not gay, she said, so I guess this is just a man thing, and I would rather have you do this, as long as it's safe, than get into any different kind of trouble you could get into on a late night out. Chris pressed Dale to tell his then-fiancée, Elaine, but Dale refused, saying that unlike the very worldly and pragmatic Sarah, Elaine would freak out if she knew, and it was better that the game stay as private as possible because outsiders couldn't really grasp its simple beauty, and though he was relieved Sarah wasn't bothered, he reminded Chris about the secrecy rule. As accustomed to the game as they were and as much sense as it made when looked at from a detached perspective, this was not an ordinary way of passing time, and the fewer people who knew about it the better. Dale was trying to make partner at his firm at a very young age and had life planned out for him: wife, kids, work, civic responsibilities, extracurricular activities. And the game would always have a place for them if they wanted it, but they should be discreet, because who knows what might happen if rumors led to misunderstandings that might not be correctable. Chris agreed, but at the next meeting, he put Dale in the tie noted above purposefully loosely to annoy him with the lack of challenge. Things got tougher and more physical as the night went on, but Chris wanted Dale to know that without him, there was no game at all, no "simple beauty." This was their game, and it was nothing all that unusual, and it had become a tradition between them, now more than ever a chance to catch up on family and career news and to cut loose and get aggressive in a still-enticing way, better than joining some work-related softball league or, worse yet, golfing, and they were honoring a history that became a new problem to solve with each new turn.

2. The Basic Deluxe. Hogtie, facedown, wrists and ankles tied together and to each other, upper arms tied together and knees bound.

This is a simple addition, but it makes escape much more difficult, because movement of the arms and legs is severely restricted. In particular it's the loop of rope that locks the upper arms together that toughens things, because it prevents flexing the elbows and moving the hands in helpful ways to help execute the key to all the ties: getting the hands loose.

Chris used this tie on Dale effectively during the latter's bachelor party, where the whole group of guys assembled were introduced to the game. (By college, one of the rules was that losing the game—not being able to get untied—meant staying in that position for the rest of the night. That didn't quite happen during the bachelor party, but Dale was helpless on the bed for quite a while, red-faced, cursing into his gag.) Chris used this tie because it was right before the stripper was scheduled to arrive at the hotel suite, and he knew Dale would go along with it, but was drunk and would lose and spend a good portion of his night on the bed while his friends enjoyed themselves, and it was a secret reminder to Dale of Chris and Dale's friendship before Dale's life changed in the eyes of God, etc. Chris was best man at Dale's wedding and had planned the whole thing, even though he knew that he would pay for it at the next game after Dale's honeymoon.

This is also the tie that, unknown to Dale, Chris had first introduced to his friend Anthony at Harvard when getting his MBA at the business school. Anthony was a tall, dark, willowy guy who could talk at length about both professional wrestling and legitimate Greco-Roman wrestling, so Chris, missing Dale on the other side of the country, thought he could try broaching the subject of the game with Anthony, who seemed hesitant when told about it but agreed to meet Chris at his apartment, where Chris had made sure all the necessary supplies were ready. It's about power, Chris told Anthony. It's an entirely physical thing. Not gay at all, but manly.

After Anthony confessed that he didn't have a clear idea of what a hogtie was, Chris showed him the rope and then lay down on the floor and talked Anthony through the process, starting with the wrists and then the ankles, and finally the ropes around the upper arms and the shins just below the knees. After that, Chris nodded toward the gag and told him to stuff the sock in and tie the bandanna with a simple knot, tight. Three loud grunts in a row would mean something was wrong, like severe loss of circulation or difficulty breathing; otherwise Anthony should let Chris struggle. Anthony was initially hesitant through this instruction and wasn't very adept at placing the knots out of reach, but the position was such that it still took Chris, at that point out of practice, twenty minutes to get free, working on the knots on his wrists first and then pulling down the rope around his arms and anticlimactically untying his knees and ankles after removing the gag. Part of the struggle was for show, to show Anthony what a great idea this was, and not gay at all, because any actual bodily contact was relegated only to the tie, and after Chris freed himself, he asked Anthony, so what do you think, and Anthony grinned and said, looks like it's my turn, and got on the bed and told Chris to do his best. Chris continued to see Anthony regularly until he returned to Milwaukee after school, but he never told Dale, not because he thought Dale would be jealous, but because Dale would think other people playing the game would be a strange thing, and when Chris had brought it up at the bachelor party the night before Dale married Elaine, he had suggested it more like a frat party prank than a historical bond, and the others had watched as Dale acquiesced and struggled furiously, grunting into his gag and disconcerting the stripper who had arrived and said she'd seen a lot, but she hadn't yet seen this, but whatever works, works.

3. *The Worm. Lying face up, arms wrapped to sides with rope and legs wrapped in similar fashion.*

This one is easy, because arm movement permits you to slide one arm up and slip it through the ropes and slide

part of the coil over your shoulder and proceed from
there. This is one of the first ties Chris and Dale used because they had seen it on TV as kids in reruns of *Wild
Wild West* and other shows, and it was occasionally used
as a game-starter, with some variations, like the wrists
tied in front of the body or behind the back. Chris was the
first to tie Dale up and was disappointed that Dale could
get free so easily, but Dale countered that he bet Chris
couldn't get untied from the same tie. That's how the
game moved from Cowboys and Indians into the Cowboy
Game, following them through school, college, and adult-
hood, save for the years apart at grad school, Chris getting
an MBA at Harvard and Dale in law school at Stanford.
As soon as both men resettled in suburban Milwaukee
and began families, the Cowboy Game started up again,
though in order to play, Chris had to tell Sarah (before he
confessed) and Dale Elaine that they were going out for
an all-night poker night and drinks at the Potawatomi Ca-
sino just west of downtown. Both Chris (an executive at a
tech company called Masterson Futures) and Dale (an at-
torney jockeying to make partner at Wallers & Fergus)
had plenty of money for gambling and only played the
Cowboy Game about once a month, so the excuse worked,
and although they were only playing monthly now, things
went smoothly.

The one time this tie was effectively challenging was
when both Chris and Dale were still ten and were being watched by Dale's much older brother, Eric, while
Dale's parents went to Chicago for the weekend. Chris
and Dale explained the game to Eric because they figured

he wouldn't care, and he didn't, and then they enlisted him in a unique challenge for them—seeing which one of them could get untied from the same tie first, which would mean Eric would have to tie them both. They were planning hogties, but there wasn't enough rope, so they asked Eric what they could do, and Eric, seeing an opportunity to have the night to himself, told them he would do it specially, with duct tape. The boys thought it would still be easy to free themselves, so they shrugged at the suggestion and went along with it. Eric wrapped it around Dale, shoulder to ankles, and then Chris the same way. He was big enough that he could lift both slim boys and place them side by side on Dale's parents' bed. Eric finished by taping both boys' mouths shut. They lay there struggling and flexing while they could hear Eric and other people making noise downstairs, and they soon realized that they would have to wait for Eric to free them, and that none of the three could confess the act out of fear of further questioning and likely punishment by their parents, not to mention retribution from Eric.

The next day they established rules: only rope could be used; the rope could be cut, but no more than fifty feet of it could be used; and the rope had to be thick enough so that the knots weren't impossible (they'd experimented once with clothesline, which was too thin), but not too thick (which made the knots too loose). If there were gags, they had to be a sock in the mouth and bandanna tied around the head to keep it in place, which they had seen on TV and with which you could still breathe through your mouth if you needed to. At least one of them had to be free at all times for safety reasons and to act as a lookout in case some quick untying needed to be done. The boys made a pact, then, that this was their game, and now it had rules, and they would test the rules out as they continued the game when they had the opportunity at either Chris's or Dale's house.

As they grew through junior and high school, those rules stayed in place, and the duct tape incident was never mentioned to anyone, and the young Chris and Dale decided not to break the informal rule about telling anyone else about the game, a rule that was easier to break for both of them than the rules about the ropes, which stayed in place, even when they were grown men with families living back in Milwaukee again.

4. The Chair Worm. Seated in a chair, arms at sides, rope wound around torso/chair back and ankles tied to chair legs.

This could potentially be easy, like the previous tie, but it depends on the chair and how the rope is dispersed. A good deal of rope, wound around the torso and chair from nearly the shoulder to the wrists tightly, makes pulling one arm up and out a more difficult task, especially if the chair is stiff-backed and heavy. Fifty feet of rope actually gets eaten up quickly, though, so that means most of the rope is spent securing the forearms to the chairs, or else one gets a thinner spread from wrists up to shoulders. Chris and Dale sometimes used chairs as kids, but had a tough time explaining why they needed to pull a kitchen or other sturdy chair into one of their bedrooms for a game. No excuse was needed, though, when it was a sleepover, and the host's parents were out for the evening. Chris and Dale were both good, obedient kids and great student-athletes and were left unsupervised by both sets of parents in high school often because the parents knew they wouldn't be up to anything worrisome, so they had free nights to play with chairs.

The only time any of the parents became aware of the game was when Chris and Dale were twelve and Dale's mother, Jane, found Chris tied this way in Dale's bedroom with Dale gagging him and demanded an explanation. Dale and Chris explained that it was just a physical challenge, and there was nothing else to it, but Jane made Dale untie Chris and swore them both to stop playing, which they promised her they would. (They'd gotten the rope from Chris's parents, saying that they needed it for a knot-tying badge in Scouts.) Neither Chris nor Dale ever heard anything else about it from any of their parents, and were more cautious after that, until they got to Cornell and had a room to themselves.

Inseparable from almost the moment Chris's family moved next door to Dale's, the boys became known in school as the Twins, and they even looked alike—slender build, dark hair (although Dale's was wavy and Chris's was straight), pale features, and blue eyes. They shared far more than the game, as kids, at Cornell, and again as adults, and although they looked less like brothers as they aged, they still acted as if they were, each closer to the other than to his own siblings. Nobody thought the friendship was uncommon at all because Dale and Chris also had plenty of other friends, and the Twins were admired for their brotherly behavior, and they weren't unlike other friends who formed close lifelong bonds, except for the game, which was theirs alone, they assumed.

Because it was such a good idea, they wondered whether other people also played it, but when Chris learned from a friend in eighth grade that being tied up was called bondage, and that it was a dirty sex thing, he reported this to Dale, and they decided that what they were doing was not a dirty sex thing, but that they should keep things secret unless they could find people to confide in, perhaps, they thought, at college, other guys to play to make it into a kind of tournament challenge. It was such a strange idea to introduce to conversation, though, that it was easy to keep mostly private, and Chris and Dale's shared passion for the struggle and release brought them even closer. When they lived on opposite coasts, they would gently prank each other by sending packages of rope, or a bandanna and a sock, that had to be hidden or quickly tossed, unless either man had to open the package in the presence of others, in which case elaborate stories would be told by either man about an old college frat joke, though neither joined a frat while at Cornell, Chris busy studying economics and Dale in pre-law. The game, though, became shorthand for their closeness, and even with jobs and families back in Milwaukee, it just took a phone call or email with the right words to induce a night of feverish play.

In their daily lives, they understood each other to be good family men, Dale with his wife, Elaine, and his daughter, Ava; and Chris with Sarah and his two boys, Jackson and Wilder; with Ava and Jackson the same age and Wilder a year younger. Chris and Dale's kids had regular play dates and eventually reached the age at which Dale and Chris had played Cowboys and Indians, and they watched but saw no sign in any of their kids of any kind of captivity game, somewhat to their relief. They both knew that since they'd managed to hide so much from their own parents, that their kids would hide, or even currently were hiding, things from them the way they still mostly hid the game, Chris and Dale, meeting monthly, or more often if possible, at the Hampton Inn, usually on a Sunday night, each bringing work clothes along so they could dress and leave for work in the morning from the motel, tired and rope-marked, but satisfied.

5. *The Chair Basic. Seated in a chair, arms tied behind the back behind the chair, ankles tied to the chair legs. Optional addition of ropes around the torso and tying the thighs down to the seat.*

This was an easier tie in standard form, because it was simply a matter of getting the wrists free, until one night, when playing with a chair that had a crossbar, Dale improvised and tied Chris's wrists down to the bottom crossbar of the chair and then the ankles together and back to the wrists, a move that limited mobility of Chris's arms and meant Dale won that night, which was freshman year at Cornell.

There were rumors at Cornell that Chris and Dale were gay and boyfriends and that they were into S&M, after

Dale made brief mention of the game to a mutual friend, but Chris and Dale assured their friends they were not gay, not that there was anything wrong with that, but just close friends, and the S&M claim was outrageous, and they had no idea how it could have started. After the rumors began late freshman year, both Chris and Dale were quick to react, Dale by finding a girlfriend he dated until the fall semester of senior year, and Chris by embarking on a very public succession of short-lived relationships and one-night stands. They also talked about it privately and wondered one night if it might be just a little gay, but they settled on the merits of the masculine struggle for power and control and the fact that there was no sexual activity during the games, though both men sometimes got unexplained erections, that it was all just good clean fun, rough play, and not gay in any way possible, because obviously they were both attracted to women and had girlfriends and so on. It was purely a power struggle, man against man, no sexual connotation at all. There was something masculine about it that precluded it being queer, they decided. It was like football to homosexuality's badminton. No contest. But while Chris never followed through with girlfriends or Sarah on the few erections he would sometimes get, mostly when doing the tying rather than being tied, Dale had an encounter at Stanford tied in this particular position that left him very self-conscious about keeping his hands away from the midsection of Chris's familiar body.

At a bar with some friends, Dale broke the secrecy rule and described a very plain version of the contest to his fellow students, emphasizing the physical, rugged side of it as an example of the crazy things someone might do as an undergrad. Later that night his classmate Thomas told Dale privately that if he was still interested in playing, that Thomas knew a guy who would be interested, to which Dale quickly said yes, even while thinking of the act almost as if he were cheating on Chris. Thomas gave him a phone number, and the next Thursday Dale arrived at Frank's apartment, having been told that Frank's roommates would be out all night and that he was eager to play.

Frank was tall, blond, and very muscular; unlike both Chris and Dale, he looked as if he almost had the strength to break the ropes merely by flexing, no untying needed. He was also calmly cheerful and enthusiastic, and motioned Dale to come in while offering him a beer. After the beer and some idle chatter about Stanford and their studies, Frank slapped the kitchen table they were sitting at and said, let's get to it, I'll tie you up first. Instead of using one of the kitchen chairs, though, Frank ushered Dale into his bedroom, where a '70s style metal office chair with a rigidly inclined vinyl back stood ready in the middle of the room. Dale took out the rope he had purchased for the night, as well as the sock and bandanna, and gave Frank basic instructions, but Frank, taking the rope, waved him off and told him he knew what to do, and joked that maybe he should gag Dale first.

Frank put all his strength into the tie described above and did it so expertly and quickly that Dale was surprised and was initially glad that the escape wouldn't be easy. Before he got a chance to start struggling, though, Frank gagged him tightly and then produced a piece of cloth he tied around Dale's eyes, saying that Dale was in for a special treat. Dale waited nervously in the chair while there was nothing but silence from Frank, until suddenly Dale felt Frank grab his ass and pull his midsection forward from the chair back and then unzip Dale's pants. Dale started to struggle furiously at this and grunt into the gag, shaking his head *no* at what was to come, but Frank just laughed and said that he had sucked off plenty of straight guys already, and that all Dale had to do was try to get free, if he wanted, or concentrate on having some extra-special fun. Dale got an erection despite himself with Frank's coaxing, and for what seemed like hours Frank alternated between masturbating him and sucking his exposed cock until it felt raw, and finally with a burst Dale came and sagged in the chair, still tied, gagged, and blind. Nothing to be ashamed of, Frank said while patting him on the shoulder, just a little horseplay, you've probably been waiting for that for years, and anyway pleasure is pleasure, though because it's so evident that you like being tied up, I think I'll leave you that way a little while longer for you to escape if you want, or just enjoy your predicament. As hard as Dale fought the tie, he couldn't free himself, and he left the apartment only hours later when finally let loose, exhausted and more ashamed of his own desire than angry at the physically imposing Frank. And he was even more ashamed of himself when a few months later he called Frank up and asked if he could come back, just once, nothing really too sexual, and Frank said sure, your pleasure's mine.

6. *The Reach. Seated in a chair that has arms, rope wound around chest, forearms tied to chair arms, ankles tied together or to the chair legs.*

Depending on the motion allowed to the upper arms, this tie is either relatively easy or completely impossible to escape, if there's no way to slide your arms backward. Without that movement, your hands have no access to any rope, and therefore can't begin the escape. When they had a chair like this, this tie was usually a late night game-ender between Chris and Dale because it was impossible to escape from, but relatively comfortable, so either Chris or Dale could stay in it for a long period. The way the game developed, sometimes the first tie of the night would be likely inescapable and a game-ender, but usually they traded easier ties a few times, drinking beer in between turns, until they decided that it was time for the more agile and quick-witted one to finish the other off. And they were near-equals at both tying and escape, so each won roughly half the time, Chris with a slightly better record than Dale. The only uncomfortable part about this tie was the gag they used (the sock and bandanna as described above), though sometimes they played without the gag, depending on how rough they wanted to get, which as undergrads was always rough.

Once Dale and Chris had both returned to Milwaukee and started families, Dale purchased a perfect chair for this at an antique store, and on nights when his daughter was at a friend's house for a sleepover, Dale (with the awkward memory of Frank) would ask his wife Elaine, more worldly than Dale originally thought, to tie him up in this way and masturbate him to climax, which she did at first only obligingly but later with greater and greater skill and enthusiasm, because of the devoted and energetic way he would repay her in bed after being untied. One night they even switched the schedule and had intense sex before the tying, so that Dale could stay tied for the rest of the night. Chris hadn't owned a chair like this since they were undergrads and had no excuse to buy one, so he was a little jealous of Dale getting extra time to struggle helplessly, even though he found the sexual aspect of it a little off-putting, enough for Chris to cool down the play for a few games and willingly lose, until he reassured himself Dale was there for the game only, the simple but fierce struggle, and he returned to full intensity.

The position was a favorite of both men, because it was so simple—the wrists weren't even bound—yet it could be a game-ender. Game-ending, when one exhausted man finally used an impossible tie on the exhausted other, was not just a display of rough physical power but rather acknowledgment of victory, since the men didn't struggle over being tied but calmly acquiesced to whatever tie the other had chosen, saving energy for the escape itself, but after a certain point each time they played, they both knew who had been the better player that night, both tying and escaping, and the losing man would submit to the game-ender as a kind of checkmate, a binding that was less about continued struggle (though of course there was some), than about who won and who lost. At Cornell the simple proclamation of the tie name "The Reach" was shorthand for indicating the game had been won, and the loser would now be tied to the chair for the rest of the allotted time. The men added other trophies as they grew and the game grew—the loser would provide the next round's beer, or do the other man's laundry, or wash his car, or owe him a certain amount of money—but the primary punishment for the loser was the extended tie, which Dale and Chris had both experienced in a variety of positions, but especially in the wooden armchair in their Cornell apartment, either man nodding off drunk after a while and waking up hours later to find himself still bound, often still gagged, and desperately needing to use the bathroom. Taunting during this state, which both men experienced often at Cornell, was part of victory, although neither man was too sadistic. The tougher task was getting the other man's attention in the morning, and Chris, after a long night during their junior year at Cornell, awoke still gagged to hear no trace of Dale and struggled so hard in the chair that he tipped himself backward, knocked his head against a side table, and lay like that for the fifteen more minutes while Dale used the toilet and took a long shower, having not heard the chair slam to the ground in Chris's room. After that, "tipping the chair" became shorthand for playing too rough, so that the men could police themselves and not get too out of hand, though senior year at Cornell, Dale once purposely tipped the chair back just to experience what it was like.

7. The Stretch. Tied spread-eagle to a bed, face up or face down, wrists and ankles tied to the frame on the four corners of the bed.

Unless the ropework is sloppy, this is very tough to escape from and almost always a game-ender, because, tied in a tight X on the bed, usually face up, there's no way to reach the knots at the bed frame and no way to use two hands together to work on knots. Success also depended on the size of the bed used; in a twin bed it might be possible for one hand to reach another, while in a king-sized bed you would be stretched taut. As a game-ender it's more uncomfortable than the armchair tie (your shoulders get sore with your arms at an upward angle), but it's still livable. Chris and Dale only used this tie infrequently, when they had access to a large bed, which neither did at Cornell, so it was a tie limited to their youth (modeled on TV images of cowboys tied spread-eagle in the desert), and then to when they started getting a room at the Hampton regularly, once both had returned to Milwaukee. The Hampton bed was king-sized and therefore serviceable, and while the tie was somewhat anticlimactic, it was an entertaining challenge for the men to stretch and bow, helplessly clutching for the rope or trying to loosen it.

And the tie was used only once in a long while after Dale felt he'd had the last straw from Chris, once. First there was the bachelor party, which was just humiliating and not sport, and then there was Chris telling Sarah about the game, which was private, shortly after their marriage, and then the last straw, when Chris emailed Dale one night to tell him that Chris had mentioned the game to two guys where he worked as a college-type sport, and they were both interested in trying it out, confident that they would both get loose, and Chris wanted to know whether Dale wanted to set up a tournament-style play at one of his friend's homes. Dale felt obliged to agree to this, but it made him furious because Dale needed to be cautious—Milwaukee was a relatively small town, and here was Chris, telling everyone he could about what was supposed to be private, a bond that he and Dale had shared since they were kids, a secret Dale had only shared once at Cornell and once at Stanford because it had slipped out while Dale was drunk. The tournament only happened once, at unmarried Josh's condo, and Chris bought extra rope for it and explained the unique rules—whoever got free first in a contest of two men would win—and both Josh and Kevin were enthusiastic about the game and not freaked out, and things went smoothly, even though Josh and Kevin were both terrible at doing the tying and getting free, and the tournament was a mess itself because it was hard to decide who should be tying whom and what winning really meant, and of course they couldn't do the game-ender on either new guy because it would be too cruel, so the tournament was not repeated (though Josh later told Chris that he and Kevin had been continuing to practice on each other). When Chris next wanted to play, Dale eagerly said yes but suggested a change of hotels, that it was Chris's turn to reserve the room, but that they should find a place with some new furniture, and Chris agreed. They decided to meet at the Holiday Inn downtown, and when the two men met there at 8 p.m., Dale was ready not just to tie but to fight.

It was his turn to begin the tie, so first he put Chris in a strenuous hogtie that it took Chris an hour to get free from, and then, after his turn, a chair tie that took another hour. After one more turn by an eager Dale, clutching and ripping at the ropes, Chris agreed to Dale's suggestion of a face-up spread-eagle on the queen-size bed they'd gotten with the room, acknowledging how ferocious Dale had been that night. Dale tied Chris down quickly and firmly, first his arms to the upper corners and then, pulling Chris toward the end of the bed by crooks of his knees to stretch Chris's arms further, tying his ankles to the lower corners. Then Chris lifted his head for the gag, and Dale stuffed in the sock and tied the bandanna tightly, before arranging a pillow for Chris to rest his head on. Then Dale told Chris not to start struggling yet because they needed to talk, though Dale would do the talking. Dale stood to Chris's left with his arms folded and told him: you're ruining our game. Dale told Chris that he had broken rules and was letting the secrecy of the game erode, and that Dale couldn't allow that, so there would be a special punishment. Dale took out his hotel key card and placed it on Chris's stomach.

What your punishment is, Dale said, is that I'm leaving now. Housekeeping will find you by about one or two o'clock tomorrow, unless management doesn't come earlier when you don't check out on time. So you have plenty of time to think, Dale told Chris, about our game and our history together, and about how you're straining our relationship and the boundaries of the game, and he hoped Chris could see his side of things, if not now then at least eventually, and that he hoped they could go back to playing like normal, like they had always played, just the two of them, intimate with each other and the game. As Chris started struggling desperately, Dale gathered his things and told him that it was fine if he got free, that he should definitely try, but that he should also think of what he was going to say to the Holiday Inn management when they found him the next day. By this point Chris was red with strain and cursing into his gag, but Dale just patted Chris on his stomach silently, smiled down at Chris staring up at him, and walked out the door. After a difficult time explaining an "old college buddy prank" to the hotel management the next day, Chris called Dale at work to scream at him about how they were done and everything was over, that he could never forgive Dale, and the two men didn't talk for about four months, until Chris, in a casual email, suggested that some revenge might be in order and it was Dale's turn to rent the room at the Hampton, and the lure of the game pulled them back together.

8. The Frozen Worm. Lying face up or sitting, wrists tied in front and upper arms tied together in back, ropes tied around the ankles and upper thighs in loops so that they are secured together.

This position can be a relatively easy one without embellishment, and depends, like most of the ties, mostly on how the wrists are tied—crossed, parallel, or facing away from each other. For Chris and Dale, the wrists were most often tied crossed to allow for more space to tie the upper arms together behind the back, but they were sometimes tied facing away, elbows as corners of a squared-off U formed by the tied wrists. This tie also left a lot of room for experimentation, using the remainder of the rope to elaborately fix the tied arms to the torso, or to turn the bound man on his stomach and tie ropes from the ankles to ropes wrapped around the shoulders. Once, at the beginning of a game at the Hampton, Chris and Dale sat together on the king-sized bed, and Dale showed Chris a collection of photos he had found on the Internet. In the pictures, naked men were tied up in incredibly elaborate ways, often with colored rope, in positions both familiar and new to the two men. The nudity was obviously something to be overlooked, but Dale said it was the ropework to consider because there was a lot there to learn for future games. Dale told Chris that they were looking at images of shibari, a Japanese form of erotic rope bondage based on, to Dale's mind, the more interesting and relevant hujujitsu, a practice in which a prisoner was bound by samurai, but no knots were used because the pretrial prisoner, who might be innocent, would be publicly humiliated if tied with knots.

Dale told Chris, as Chris flipped through the desktop-printed Internet photos, that shibari was both a gay and a straight thing, and that in trying to do some research to liven up the game (they were in their early forties by this point and had been playing for over three decades), he stumbled across them on the Internet. Chris was fascinated and wanted to know more, as well as try things out during the game, but asked Dale, why so many images, some of them obviously not reproducible under the fifty-foot limit, and Dale just shrugged and said that he thought it would inspire them, and that even though some of them were erotic, that wasn't the point, and, shuffling through the pages, he pulled out a few ties he thought they could adapt as game-enders, because they looked comfortable, or at least the men in the photos looked comfortable in them. It had never occurred to Chris that what they were doing was parallel to a traditional practice completely unknown to them, though he knew about what Dale did with his wife, but not about Frank at Stanford. To Chris, and to Dale, to a certain extent, what they had been doing with each other was pure sport, like the soccer and track they were involved with in high school and college. Except the game was, essentially, theirs alone, and they had grown skilled with each others' bodies and knew how far each others' elbows and knees bent, and how thick each others' wrists and ankles were. They always played fully clothed, of course, usually in casual clothes but sometimes in their work clothes if it was an anniversary of the game, like the anniversary of being tied up by Eric, or when their first all-nighter at Cornell occurred, and the men chose that night to celebrate.

Chris couldn't quite understand the reason for the nudity in the photos, or else he told Dale he didn't understand how what they did could be erotic, and Dale agreed with a little too much enthusiasm, saying that what he and Chris did was more like hujujitsu but better. Chris asked Dale whether there was anything in the photos in particular he wanted to try because it was Dale's turn to tie first the night he shared the photos, and that's how Dale directed Chris to the way the legs were tied folded, which made its way into the tie described above, as well as some of the wrapping around the shoulders, because he and Dale had been trying for years to think of a way to make escape difficult, even once either of them got his wrists untied, and Dale said that some of the wrapping and looping in the photos might make arm movement difficult, even with wrists free, so Chris nodded approvingly and they studied the pictures, pointing things out to each other for a half-hour before they each pounded a beer and Chris got on the bed, ready for Dale to get to work. Dale's second try at Chris, which was a variation of the above tie, secured the elbows to the torso so well that, even once Chris got his wrists untied, he couldn't free his elbows and unwrap his shoulders or reach the knots around his legs, so the position ended up being a game-ender, and for the first time in decades, they found themselves having to make a new rule—whether the bound man should be left in his half-untied state or whether he should be put back into the original position for the rest of the night.

Lying on the bed after struggling for an hour and grunting for the gag to be removed, Chris told Dale he couldn't believe they'd never come across this before, and that he was glad Dale had found the photos, because the standard positions had been thoroughly explored, but he hesitated when Dale suggested that Chris's wrists be retied. Dale reminded him of the night at Cornell he spent on his back hugging his knees to his chest, his wrists tied to his ankles in a position called "The Bundle," and told Chris that it's the original tie that's the game-ender, and that he couldn't do much with his arms anyway, so the tie should be restored, and after a quiet minute of Chris closing his eyes and considering it, and Dale sitting on the bed next to him watching him think, Chris said yes, it would be correct that his wrists should be retied because he'd lost the game and needed to fully suffer the consequences. The new rule, then, was that partial untying without escape meant that the original tie should be restored as punishment.

After sliding Chris over to the right half of the bed and placing a pillow under his head, Dale retied his wrists, not tightly but firmly, but waited until after he'd gotten ready for bed to gag Chris, jokingly telling him, *goodnight, sweet dreams,* like he always did when he won, before turning off the lights and crawling into bed next to Chris, the two old friends lying side by side, drifting off into sleep as best they could, until the wakeup call at 6 a.m., when Dale untied Chris, and without needing to talk much, the two men got dressed for work and drove to one of several nearby restaurants for the post-game breakfast they always shared, and then parted with knowing smiles and headed back to their ordinary work week and their families and their comfortable lives, until they both decided it was time to play again.

ACKNOWLEDGEMENTS

Thank you to the editors of the following publications in which some of this work first appeared: *Bare Fiction*, the *Blue Lake Review*, *Caketrain*, *Conjunctions*, *Guernica*, *Hobart*, and *Milk*.

Thank you to Peter Blewett, Mary Blewett, Charu Malik, Henri Rozier, Peter Gadol, Jen Hofer, and Matias Viegener for unwavering support and encouragement. Thank you to Joe Milazzo, Janice Lee, and Eric Lindley for more or less the same reasons, plus sage editorial advice. Thank you to Matt McGowan for putting up with me. Thank you to Callie Collins and Jill Meyers for your belief in my work.

Thank you to Will Lingle for being Will Lingle.

Thank you especially to Lesley and Rowan Grider.

Thank you, mom.

ABOUT A STRANGE OBJECT

A Strange Object is a small press and literary collective established in 2012 and based in Austin, Texas. A\SO believes in surprising, wild-hearted fiction, diverse voices, and good design across all platforms. *Misadventure* is A Strange Object's second book. Learn more at astrange object.com.